DIXIE

Book Two: Ramble On

A Novel by Sybil Watters

Printed and bound in the United States of America

First printing • ISBN 978-0-9998884-9-0

Copyright © 2018

Discover the latest in the **DIXIE Series** and purchase exclusive merchandise:
www.dixiebookseries.com

Like and follow Author Sybil Watters on Facebook
www.facebook.com/SybilWatters

Or via Twitter
@SybilWatters

Editor: Erinn Giblin: Yours Truly, The Editor

TO ORDER ADDITIONAL COPIES VISIT:

www.scottpublishingcompany.com/store

SCOTT COMPANY PUBLISHING
P.O. Box 9707 • Kalispell, MT 59904
Toll Free: 1-800-628-0212
Fax: 1-406-756-0098

For

the people who strike a match

to burn it all down

and

unexpectedly create a phoenix.

ACKNOWLEDGMENTS

To my Swiss dad, who doesn't speak proper English, certainly doesn't understand southern slang, and has admonished me for using it. He's cool with the cursing, though.

To Bravo, Elvis, Lady and Henry, my rescue dogs, who read and speak better English than my dad. I wish they could curse.

PROLOGUE

In his signature alpha move, Dixie drew his coarse face into John's until his eyes were piercing through to the back of John's skull and beads of sweat, trickling from the tip of his nose, could be felt and tasted on Dixie's cracked lips.

"Now you gonna git yur li'l wife to git me what I want, and you gonna git it done by next week," he huffed into John's mouth. "I want one of them biker boys, don't care which one, sittin' in front of me. I know Billy, and I know him all too well. He may be gettin' along with those guys right good, but there is bound to be one of 'em that can't stand him. I'll take any of 'em though. We come from the same stock." John writhed a bit but stayed in the uncomfortable space of Dixie's words. "Tell me ya hearin' what I'm sayin' to ya," Dixie demanded as he looked back over one shoulder, then the other. "You gonna end up like ol' man Dan if ya ain't…now wasn't that a sad state?"

John understood, of course. Everyone within those concrete walls understood what happened to ol' man Dan, especially John, his celly. And everyone understood the State's suicide explanation would stand, and nothing would be done of it. One less chicken, one strong hen to rule the roost. It was working that way, and nobody on the outside cared enough about ol' Dan what's-his-name to ask questions.

John had forced the bloody memories of the fork, the sheets, and the salad that had become of ol' man Dan's wrists far from his mind. Until that moment when Dan's name spat from Dixie's mouth into his. Then the horrid scene and the fear gushed over the dam of his mental blockade. He squeezed his eyes shut.

"What's the matter boy, ya scared? Look at me. LOOK AT ME!"

John opened his eyes again and would swear Dixie's gaze went red with rage. "I'm hearin' what y'ur sayin'. I'll git it done. She'll git one here," he promised, not knowing how to deliver.

A smirk slowly crawled across Dixie's face as he released John's shirt from his dead man's grip and eased back into a relaxed posture. "Ya will, Johnny boy. Ya will."

****

"Give me an adventure and I'll ride it."

~*Melissa Auf der Maur*

CHAPTER ONE

With his eyes locked on Dixie in the rear-view, Billy pulled the car to the dirt on the side of the road. Kathleen drew in a breath.

"What're ya doin?" Billy looked at her and back at the kids. "Billy, say sumthin'…what're ya doin?" Kathleen repeated.

"Daddy, why we stoppin'?" Buddy chimed in.

Billy glanced to the rear-view again. Dixie was closing in. "Hold up in here," he said as he swung his door open.

"BILLY!" Kathleen yelled after him.

Billy eased around to the back of the car and

propped his weight against the trunk as he lit a smoke, squinting into the sun and his soon-to-be visitor. Dixie's car crawled to a stop just inches from Billy's legs. They gazed at one another pointedly for a good thirty seconds before Dixie got out and lit a cigarette of his own. He strolled past Billy to the front driver's side window, leaning down for a better view. "Hey there. Y'all are goin' somewhere?"

Kathleen shifted away from him in her seat, inching her conscious from the weight of his hollow eyes. Her stomach heaved as he turned his gaze to the backseat and smiled towards the kids.

Billy was beside him before he could finish whatever sinister thought was ready to spew from his lips. "What ya want, Dixie?"

Dixie seemed startled by Billy's invasion of his personal space and plan, but Billy knew better. Nothing startled Dixie... even when it did.

"I dun told ya, ya best be leavin'. Just come to make sure ya was listenin'. Looks like ya listen good, Wild. Ya always did." Dixie took another pull off his cigarette and, true to form, blew the remnants of his lungs into Billy's face. "Ya know, I'm thinkin' I didn't say nuthin' 'bout takin' y'ur family with ya though."

"Not sure I know what ya mean. Of course I'm takin' my family." Billy felt the knife begin to twist in his gut. He knew it wasn't enough that he had done what Dixie said, and it might just be all the better for him that way. Dixie wouldn't have it go that easy. That would defeat the purpose of his rule and the perception of his reign.

"I said *ya* best be leavin'," Dixie said again in an even tone as his pointer finger dug into Billy's sternum, in personal indication.

As the anger rose within him at the counter-invasion

of his own personal space, Billy understood. He would be leaving, and he would be leaving his family. Leaving was not an easy thing to do, but it was a hell of a lot easier with the people he loved most. This was his home, and he had been settled. Finally. Dixie wouldn't have it that way, and Billy now knew it to be the cold, hard, end-all, be-all truth.

Billy threw his cigarette on the ground, nodded his head, and moved around Dixie to the door handle. "This goin' come back around," he said, slumping into the seat. "This goin' come back around. Just like I done told ya before."

Dixie chuckled, "So ya always say. I doubt it, Wild. Now git."

CHAPTER TWO

Kathleen watched Billy as he drove, swinging the car back towards the direction from which they had come, and she knew. As the tears spilled down her cheeks, she knew it would be goodbye. Again. Billy did not speak. He answered no questions, even as the kids chimed in "where we goin'?" and "why we goin' backwards, Daddy?"

They pulled back into the driveway they had just abandoned, and Kathleen immediately got out of the car and began pulling bags from the trunk and placing them on the ground. Billy helped her, knowing she knew everything that was coming without him having to say a word.

He put his hand on hers as she grabbed the kids' bag. "It ain't like I'll be gone forever. This will pass, Kathleen, and I'll be back before ya can say 'spit'."

Kathleen looked at him with cloudy eyes. "Will ya?" She yanked the bag out of the trunk and headed for the house. She stopped on the porch, looked over her shoulder, and nodded towards the ones who held her together. "You be tellin' y'ur children what's 'bout to happen to them now. And do it fast, before they throw a fit not knowin'."

The kids had already started to stir, of course, thinking they were just picking up something they forgot or stopping back by to meet someone for whatever reason it may be. Saying goodbye was the best any of them could come up with.

Billy stood behind the open trunk for a minute, digesting Kathleen's words, *"what's 'bout to happen to them now"*. He rested his hands on the trunk lid and glanced over his shoulder. With a sigh, he spit and slammed the trunk closed before making his way around to the open passenger side door. Leaning down, he put his best face on for posterity. "Hey now. Y'all need to help y'ur mama git this stuff in the house. Looks like you'll be stayin' back here for a bit," he said, heading up to the house with a handful. He saw Buddy's face melt as though the words had slapped him straight up.

"Noooooooooo," Buddy wailed. "Daddy you ain't goin' nowhere without meeeeeeeeee!"

"Git on out this car and git right boy. Be a man now and stop that nonsense," Billy said as he looked April and Jo over. April was collecting herself, as she always did, and preparing to collect Buddy as well. Jo simply looked out the window while she clenched her jaw. She refused to acknowledge him. Jo was bull-headed, after all, and she would hold this against him, he knew.

"That's right, Buddy. Let's git," April said, taking his hand and leading him out of the car.

Billy looked at Jo, still stoic, refusing to budge until

her stubborn stance had run its course. "I know ya hate me right now, girl. But it's what has to be. Can't none of us change it. It just is. So, git on out of this car and help y'ur mama. She needs you."

"She needs *you*, "Jo spat as she got out of the back seat, shoving past Billy with purpose.

Her words cut deep. They were true. Just as true as his had been. Kathleen needed him, but he had to go. There wasn't a damn thing anyone could do about it.

Kathleen didn't come back outside, so Billy finished bringing items to the porch for the kids and took a long, hard look at the one bag left in the trunk—his own. It was perfunctory. And sad. All by itself, when just moments before it was surrounded by things that were treasured and loved, same as he was. He felt a cold hurt sweep through him, and gravity seemed to sink him harder than normal. This was it, and *it* had been so very different only moments before.

CHAPTER THREE

He found her sitting on the bed, expressionless, staring at the wall they had planned on forgetting only a short moment before.

"I'll be back, ya hear? And I'll be sure ya git taken care of and looked after while I'm gone," Billy said in a way he, himself, didn't even find soothing.

"Ya always do," she said, never taking her eyes off the wall. "Ya better go. I know that man won't let up 'til ya do…even then…and I don't want him 'round my kids."

Billy swung his arms around her. "Shhhh, Kathleen. He'll be leavin' us alone. He'll be leavin' ya alone. I'm gonna make damn sure of it."

"Looks like he is the one makin' damn sure of things in this house," she said without hesitation or hold back.

Billy pulled away, squaring her shoulders towards him with his firm grasp. "I'm gonna make this right. Ya hear? I'm gonna make this fast and right." Her shoulders slumped in his grip as she looked down. "Okay, Billy. If ya say so."

Her disbelief was thick. She no longer trusted that he could protect them or take care of them the way he always had. No matter what had come before or what might lay ahead, he always leaned on the fact that Kathleen knew he had her and the kids protected and provided for. He choked back what purported to be tears and cleared his throat.

"Might be best if you and the kids go take up with Jamie for a while".

Kathleen nodded. "Yeah, ya know Billy, I don't really wanna be stayin' here without ya again. 'Sides, the kids will have someone to play with. Might make them miss their daddy less," she said, cutting him on purpose.

"I didn't plan this, Kathleen. Didn't even see it comin'."

Kathleen rose from the bed and started out the bedroom door to gather the things they had already returned to their house and let the kids know they were, in fact, headed out after all. "'Cept in the rearview?"

The question had been rhetorical, of course. An actual and true statement, to be sure. Meant to mean more than one thing. He got them both.

Billy took a moment, in the silence and solace of their room, to gather himself and prepare for where he was going. He figured he would leave the car with Kathleen and the kids, which only meant one destination at this point. He would have to visit Coop and visit him fast, lest he get Coop in some kind of mess himself.

Emerging from the bedroom he hugged Kathleen, kissed her, and turned to the kids, all eyes on him except for Jo. "I'm goin' for some milk. I'll be back." And he was gone. On foot.

The silence of his absence was deafening.

CHAPTER FOUR

He pulled open the screen door and knocked when he couldn't find Coop in the yard, in the garage, or around the back of the house tinkering or toying with any of his latest projects. He thought it a bit odd Coop wasn't out and about and more than a bit odd that the front door was not open to let the breeze flow in through the screen as it had been every single time he had ever visited, best he could remember. He had heard rumblings through town that Coop had taken to drinking a lot, but Billy knew Coop had taken to drinking long ago. He just never left the yard, so why would anyone else know? Unless they had business with Coop same as Billy. He didn't think anything of that chatter. It was just something else for people to talk about who usually barely knew their elbow from their ass when they got to talking. Of that, Billy knew first hand.

When Coop didn't answer his rapping the first time, Billy yelled out as he beat the door with the back of his fist the second. "Coop! It's Billy. Wake up and open up!" Billy listened until he heard stirring inside.

The wooden door cracked open a sliver, and Donna showed half her face. "Coop's sleepin' right now, Billy," she said in a soft tone.

"I'm sorry, Donna. I gotta talk to him, and I gotta talk to him now. Can't wait 'til he decides to git up. Not this time." He found it odd she hadn't opened the door on up and talked with him square on.

She looked back over her shoulder, still holding the door only slightly ajar, and then back to Billy. "A'ight then, I guess I'll go git him for ya."

She closed the door as she left, and Billy was slightly taken aback. This house had always been open. To just about anyone and everyone who wanted or needed to swing by. On top of that, Billy couldn't remember a time Donna had been his first way of introduction to the property, the house, to conducting "business" with Coop. As a matter of fact, he couldn't remember a time she even bothered to insert herself at all. He walked slowly to the porch swing, pondering the situation, as if he had nothing better to think on.

He heard the grumblings of Coop before he saw him emerge from the house, noticeably closing the door behind him. He looked worn slick, but then Billy had just woken him from a nap.

Coop walked crookedly to the swing and sat down next to Billy. He pulled a flask from his overalls and took a swig, reaching the shooter out when he was done, an offering of hot solace. Billy wasn't sure if it was the flask or Coop himself, but he could smell that clear fire all over the place. He took the flask and shot one back, politely.

"What say, Coop?"

"What say? You tell me. Heard ya done been run up outta here."

Billy almost laughed, and might have if his heart wasn't involved. "Looks like I'll be leavin' for a bit. But I'll be back."

"Ya sure of them words Billy?" Coop looked at him, eyes bloodshot and glassy.

"Ah, yeah, I'm sure. Sure as I'm sittin' next to ya right now," he said, smiling. "I ain't here to chit chat though. I need somethin' to drive."

"Well ain't that a shock. Billy Pierce needs somethin' to drive," Coop grunted and took another hard slug from the flask. "I reckon I got somethin' for ya. Seen anything ya like?"

Billy knew then that Coop had not been asleep. He had just been inside. Which was now, a certain oddity. But he had no time for details and wasn't sure he needed or wanted the extra baggage anyhow. "I might have. That Rambler back there…she got a story? She drive?"

"Now how did I know that was goin' to be the girl for you? Yeah, she drives, Billy boy. She drives good.

"Let's git to it. Ain't no sense waitin'," Billy said.

Coop looked into his eyes and said, "Ain't no sense in that 'tall".

Clearly, Coop knew the situation Billy was in. All the same, he didn't ask questions and didn't want to. Common set of ways and means, both figured. They walked around the back of Coop's house in silence, taking in the heat and the hurry. The Rambler sat glistening like a mint pearl in the sun. Even if Billy hadn't needed her that day,

15

he would have wanted her still. She was sleek, edged up, and pleasing to the eye. He felt her lines as he rounded her hood. Coop opened her up for a good look.

Not bad, Billy thought. "You got some keys for this gem?" If she fired right up, or even fired up at all, he would have her and be on his way. She did, of course. It was a rare occasion that Coop would even show any car in his back lot of a yard that wasn't going to be of some use or purpose.

"I'll be goin' then. And I'll be takin' her with me when I do," Billy announced and slipped a wad into the front pocket of Coop's overalls. He knew her worth, and he knew Coop's, so he may have overdone it a little. But Coop had been so good to him over the years, and he wasn't looking quite the same. Billy figured a little cash couldn't hurt. Coop didn't bother to check the wad. He was in no shape for counting cash.

It was almost an enjoyable experience, but this time, Billy's purchase was tainted by its complete and absolute necessity and the direction in which the Rambler would be taking him—away.

CHAPTER FIVE

He sat in the car for a good ten minutes before he started her up. Coop watched him for about three, in silence, taking pulls from the flask before he tired himself of wondering and headed back to the front of the house. Billy didn't notice he was being watched. His mind was so far off, and his heart was so far down. He wanted to go back to the house, to get Kathleen and the kids, and just head out, but all that was just not possible, and he knew it. Dixie's arms stretched far and wide, and while he may have played local, he lived broad.

Texas, Billy thought to himself as he started the engine. *Nah, that ain't where I'm goin'.*

He didn't stop on the way out of small-town Georgia, didn't acknowledge anyone on the road as folks normally did when they passed by. He didn't say any good-byes. The fewer people who knew when he left and where he was headed, the better. He wasn't even going to tell Kathleen until he thought the time was right. Right now, she thought he was headed to Texas because that had been the plan. And if pressed, that's really all she would know. When Dixie stopped them on the road and changed their plans, they were headed west for the booming construction business. She had already told her sisters, of course, and those hens chattered. One person in Kathleen's family knew something, and everybody in town knew by the end of the day if not sooner. Billy reckoned that's why they didn't come around much. Too many stories had been told and not enough secrets kept. Or maybe they didn't want to know the secrets so as not to tell them. The second explanation seemed less likely to Billy, knowing them.

All the same, Billy thought maybe those broad arms of Dixie's might catch a flutter on the wind of something, somehow, like he always did, and while Billy was doing what he was told to do, he didn't plan on things staying the way they were. And he knew Dixie knew that much about the entire situation, already. Dixie knew Billy all too well. Headstrong and proud, wild and free. Wasn't exactly the type to just do and shut up about it. Billy was a lot like Dixie in that way, but unlike him in ways that Dixie couldn't stand. Everyone knew it. And as much as Dixie felt he had done for Billy, he felt a sense of failure in Billy's right-mindedness. Sure, Billy didn't always make the right decisions. He made horrible decisions more often than not. But there was a good in him that Dixie did not possess. The good that made him stand up to the man who constantly kept him headed in the wrong direction—straight to hell.

****

He would head south through the bare, barely and currently building parts of Georgia until he hit I-75, and he would let it take him to and through Florida. To where, exactly, he wasn't quite sure. But he was sure Florida was where he wanted to be, now that his mind had been changed. He could find work, it wasn't even a care on his mind. He could and would do just about anything he came across to make ends meet, and he knew there were opportunities on this route other than throwing up houses, should the need arise. Many a story had made its way into his lock box back when he was running shine. Seems there were up and coming runs to be had, and they weren't anything to be hauling by the drink. He first heard about and saw the ghost powder with Dixie and crew, of course, and the shine runners who did talk, well… they talked a lot. About money, mostly. And there was apparently a hell of a lot more money to be made making bigger and longer runs for the seekers of the clean dust. He would think on these things as he high-tailed out of Georgia. And he would judge himself ever so slightly for already considering the evil he may pursue if times were to get tight. But Kathleen and the kids needed him, and that was just all there was to it. *Whatever it takes.*

It could have been a straight shot, an easy go, no time at all kind of trip, but Billy had taken his time on purpose, stopped and slept in the car here and there, whenever his eyes got tired. Even if it had only been a couple of hours. The weight of the words and the world he had left in the rearview were enough to knock him out cold. If a person could sleep their troubles away, Billy had started to try.

He had been in and out so many times, Billy didn't even know what time it was or what day he had left when he caught sight of it. A small watering hole with no windows and a few bikes out front in what seemed like the middle of nowhere, just past the Georgia-Florida line. She was a rough old bitch without a name, boasting a rusted metal door and black smudges on the white brick, but he was thirsty. Not that any appearance would have stopped him from going in. She may have been a no-name bitch, but she was also a palace compared to the Hawk Top, being at least three times larger in size. He was happy for the break. From driving through the constant longing to sleep and the thinking. Although the latter seemed to move the former along quicker and easier. It was hard to feel like he was moving fast when he didn't even know where he was headed.

He stretched hard and full out when he got out of the car. He lit a cigarette and paced around the dirt lot, taking in the heavy, wet heat, looking over the bikes to mentally stimulate himself enough to quell the lonely sense of nothingness he felt in his gut, until he made his way to the metal door and swung her open. Just as he expected, the sun from outside was bright enough to make the bar seem like a dungeon. He had been in many similar places, the room, the smell, the dim lighting, the smoke—all remembrances of times gone by—and somehow yet to come. He stood, letting his eyes come to, scanning the scene. The three leather clad men sitting around a round low-top near the only pool table all turned in Billy's direction and watched him as he slowly saddled up to the bar.

"What's the strongest ya got?" Billy asked the weathered, balding bartender as he made his way over, cigarette hanging from his lips.

His eyes squinted as he pulled on the cigarette and then crushed it out in the plastic ashtray near Billy's barspace. He leaned on the bar. "Well, the strongest I have isn't behind this bar," he said, cutting his eyes over to the men at the table.

Billy looked over his shoulder, trying to figure out what he was missing, if anything. He needed a shot, to start. "I need a strong drink. If that wasn't clear the first time."

The bartender stood up, chuckled a bit, "Well, I'll

be. Got myself a real man here. Nobody comes into this bar with that attitude anymore. I like it."

Billy watched as he went for the liquor on the shelves. He finished his own smoke, looking in the mirror on the wall across the bar. Some ad for some beer he had never even heard of. The bar was full of them. And the men. They just kept looking his way.

The bartender shot the high-ball glass, a triple if Billy was guessing, down the bar towards him with a nod. "Name's Tom. Yell at me if you need anything else."

Billy held up his glass and tipped it in gratitude. "Billy."

He saw Tom nod at the men. Some sort of "it's all good" gesture was the best Billy could make of it. It was a remote place, and they probably got some shady folks in and out on the regular. *Makes sense.*

He was about two and a half drinks in when one of the men from the table pulled up a stool next to him. "You play pool, stranger?"

"Mmm-hmmm," Billy said coolly.

"Well then, let's have some fun. We were about to play a game but only have three. Need a fourth."

Billy looked him over, leather from head to toe, steel kicks on the front of his boots, the lethal kind. He shot back the last of his drink. "A'ight then."

"Damn boy. That's one hell of an accent. Where are you from?"

Billy felt a searing in the hole of his heart that had been left by the answer to that very question. "I ain't from nowhere in par-ticular," he said, splitting the word in two.

The man grew a smile and responded to Billy while

looking over at his friends, "Perfect. Neither are we."

As they walked towards the others and the pool table, Billy noticed the patch surrounded by title on the back of the stranger's jacket. *Outlanders.* The flaming wheel, the skull, it was nothing less than notorious, and he was shit stuck in with it now.

CHAPTER SIX

The others were of the same origin, same colors. They, too, wore the mark of belonging. Each the same leather jacket with club patch on the back and various other patches and pins attached to the front. Billy knew those colors belonged to the Outlanders and were certainly held sacred by these obvious members. He had a strange affinity for the patch, though. It was a deviant and hellish looking empty skull, faced dead-on, with spokes emerging from its eyes and mouth that extended out to the motorcycle wheel that surrounded it. Flames erupted from the wheel inside the semi-circle insignia, "Outlanders". It was a threatening patch, to be sure, but Billy found the entirety of it, inclusive of many thoughts he, himself, had pondered. In it, he saw life, death, danger, destruction, understanding, and wrath. He wouldn't mention it, of course. Nobody in their right mind would verbally deconstruct the patch.

They removed their coats down to their sleeveless cuts, tattoos blazing, to shoot a round of pool with the stranger from the bar they had funneled through both the bartender and their own man until they found him acceptable. Billy would play a solid round with them, and they would demand another and another until Billy knew it wouldn't be daylight when the door opened, if it ever did, and he would be right drunk. The men were entertaining, for sure. Listening to them was enough to keep his brain in the moment and his heart off the table.

After four rounds of pool, a variety of tasteless jokes and stories, and a number of drinks you couldn't count if you wanted to, the man to first approach Billy at the bar blurted, "I don't think we ever got your name."

"Don't reckon ya did," Billy said, slamming the q-ball into the break, causing three others to sink into the table.

They all stood looking at him, silent. Billy looked back at them. "What?"

They hissed with laughter. "Boy, you are something else. I guess that wasn't clear enough. What's your name?"

"Billy."

"Well. Billy, sure glad to meet you. I'm Hatchett." He smacked the shorter guy on the shoulder. "This one here's Troll, on account of his ugly mug, and our buddy taking a piss, that's Henry-Nine, Niner for short...if you haven't noticed..."

Billy knew what he meant. "Henry-Nine", as they called him, was missing a finger. Of course he wouldn't ask why or how. "Them's some int'resting God-given names y'all got there," Billy responded.

Troll stepped forward, and Hatchett pushed him back, admonishing him. "He didn't mean anything by it, little man. Settle down. He knows." Pausing, Hatchett looked back to Billy. "Isn't that right, Billy?"

Billy thought on it. Of course, he knew. Everyone knew, or at least knew something, about the Outlanders. So-called outsiders, non-natives, belonging to some other culture—true to definition. They were serious and not to be messed with. Billy knew that. "Reckon I do."

Hatchett smiled. "Thought so. Interesting meeting you here. We were just discussing how we needed some new…talent for a few odd jobs, and here you are, talking about racing cars. You said you were headed to Florida. You are in Florida. How far did you plan on going?"

"Ain't quite sure on that. Best I can tell, I'll stop when I feel like I'm there."

Henry-Nine came out of the bathroom, zipping up his pants as he did, and they all turned to look at him. "What'd I miss?"

Hatchett pointed in Billy's direction. "Billy here is headed as far and as fast as he can go in Florida, or at least as far as he can go until he 'gits' there," he said with Billy's accent. They all laughed.

"That funny?" Billy asked, half pointedly.

Again, Troll shifted forward, and again, Hatchett stopped him. "I like you, Billy. I'm just yanking your chain on that slang. Let's talk some more about where you are headed. I have some ideas for you," he said, looking first to Henry-Nine then back to Troll. The latter seemed like a courtesy.

Troll seemed angry. "Hatchett, you don't know this

25

guy from any other asshole that walks into a bar."

"Oh, but I do," was all Hatchett said as he walked right past him to their table. "Take a seat, Georgia boy. We got some things to discuss. Don't mind him," he nodded towards Troll. "He has eaten asphalt one too many times... or that's an excuse we use."

Billy laughed in Troll's direction, which clearly angered him. Figuring he wasn't all the way to rip-roaring drunk because he recognized he had all the time in the world—this world anyway—he obliged and sat down to talk to Hatchett about whatever "ideas" he may have. He had just crossed the Georgia-Florida line, and here he was already crossing the line, and he knew it. "I was admirin' y'ur bikes out front. Them's some hot wheels."

Hatchett perked up. "You like those? Well, you should. They aren't bar jumpers if you know what I mean." It was a half statement, half question, directed at Billy to gauge his understanding of their culture, their purpose, and their governance.

"Bar jumpers...ahhh yeah, I reckon' I do. Had me a few on four wheels in my day. He knew enough to know they didn't ride just any bike all over the place, and a bar jumper was the same as his favorite cars, even though he drove them into the ground, quite literally. The jumpers were more extreme bikes designed to ride from bar-to-bar, or on other short trips. And Billy got the feeling they were a long way from home.

Hatchett was pleased. What do they call you back home, Billy? Because you sure don't seem like a proper Billy to me."

Billy laughed. "Wild...they call me Wild."

Well, then *Wild*, here's to you. Hatchett raised a shot glass and threw it back.

****

They carried on and on, through the night best Billy could tell without windows. He felt as though he had known Hatchett and Henry-Nine all his life. Troll was different. He couldn't figure what the problem was, but he had known many a man like him, and the others didn't seem to pay him as much mind as they should have either. They weren't going to have a problem. Of that, Billy was sure. When Troll left to relieve himself for what seemed like the twentieth time, Billy asked the others openly, "What the fuck's his problem?"

"Ahhh, Troll's always got a problem. He doesn't like...people. Mostly. He's a pain in the ass, but he's our brother."

"He done gone to the pisser 'bout twenty times," Billy pointed out.

Niner leaned in and looked at Hatchett, who nodded once. "He ain't pissin'."

Billy thought about what Niner had said and caught on in a flash. "Well, shit. I guess he ain't so bad after all. Thought maybe he was a leaker or sumthin'."

They were roaring at his comment when Troll came back from the can. "What's so funny?"

"Had to be here," Hatchett said quickly.

Troll's disproportionate face grew even more ugly. "I AM here. What's so damn funny?"

Niner took over, "Nothing any of us could re-tell right, Troll. Now, shut up."

Troll looked to the three of them, shook his head as though in disagreement, and left it alone as he went to grab another beer at the bar. Billy recognized the hierarchy.

They were ripe with rules and rank, and Troll wasn't much for the first, but he was tied to the second.

Billy meant to cut the silence at the table, "Hey, say, where the hell are we anyway?"

Hatchett and Niner lost a loud laugh. Billy looked at them seriously. "What?"

"You been here for hours and hours. We know where you come from, where you've been, your life story, and you are just now telling us you have no clue where you are in this very minute?"

Billy thought on that for longer than a moment. His *life-story*. He had made sure they didn't know his life story, but they knew enough. After the long silence, Hatchett leaned forward. "You sure you know where you are...up here?" he said, tapping a finger on Billy's head. They all laughed this time. Even Troll. *Little shitstick*, Billy dubbed him silently.

"Jasper," Hatchett blurted.

Billy looked over his shoulder for another person.

"Jasper, Florida, you jackass! You asked where you were. Damn boy, maybe time to ease up. But that's not how we do it, is it boys? This one's about to pass out, which means it's time to crank it up!"

Tom brought another round of whiskeys when he heard the words. Billy noticed they had their own language and dialogue that was comprised of few words and a lot of gestures. He wondered what business they had in a small space like Jasper, Florida, but he knew not to ask. He figured they knew it and knew it well, though, based on their relationship with Tom. If business was on the table, Billy would bet it had something to do with the rush Troll kept seeking out in the bathroom.

Hatchett watched Billy closely. He liked the way Billy talked, and Hatchett could tell Billy had been though some shit—had done some shit. He'd found himself a perfect potential…something. What that something was, he wasn't quite sure yet.

"I want to see you drive. I believe you may be as good as you say you are."

Billy would always accept that invitation, and when it sounded like a challenge, he couldn't grab the keys fast enough. But he was in no state. "A'ight. I believe I'm gonna need a few blinks 'fore I can throw her 'round, y'all. Where can I find a bed in *Jasper*," he said with emphasis on the last word for kicks.

Niner and Hatchett laughed. "I like you. So, I'll let you in on a little secret. There's a room back behind this bar where you can sleep it off. We'll catch you when you decide you're done blinking."

Troll leaned forward and whispered into Hatchett's ear. Hatchett responded out loud, "That isn't any club business, Troll. Mind your own. Maybe you should go to bed too," he said in a sarcastic tone.

Tom showed Billy the bunk room, and for Billy, it was an immediate lights out.

CHAPTER SEVEN

Kathleen decided the minute Billy left that she would make the most normal life for their kids that she could. Kathleen, too, had changed her plans. She wasn't going to Jamie's. She wasn't jostling the kids around anymore than she had to. *Not anymore.* She would maintain the status quo, if there ever really was one. She had always wanted the best for all of them, together, as she knew Billy did. But she and Billy were different creatures. He had gotten himself into the thick of things he couldn't quite get out of, even though they had come so close. She put the kids to bed that night. The girls had gone easy, but Buddy stopped her, grabbing her arm as she kissed his forehead.

"Daddy said he was goin' for milk, Mama. It's dark now. Where'd he go to git it?"

31

"Don't you worry, Buddy. Daddy will be back," was all she said. She tucked his blanket and left the room, closing the door behind her before she broke down and cried. She knew, of course, that milk was not the mission and Billy would not be back for quite some time. There was Dixie to think of first and, of course, whatever Billy would get into where he was going to think of second.

She had no worries that money would come from that place, but she had enough memories, and intimate knowledge of the man she had married twice, to know that he got distracted easily, despite his intentions. She wasn't dumb enough to think he would carry on with their family plan of moving to Texas to rebuild their life, not with threats looming overhead, but she was pained to realize, at this very moment, she had no clue where Billy was, where he might be headed, and what was in his mind, exactly. He had just gotten right. *They* had just gotten right. The kids were settled. *Damn that Dixie Bates.* And she knew he was watching. Watching her, watching the house, ear to the ground on Billy's whereabouts, knowing full well Billy wouldn't tell her a thing because of it. Just another way for him to hurt them, she figured. Divide and conquer.

Kathleen did what she knew to do. She got down on her knees and prayed. She prayed for the safety of her family, for the right mind of her husband, and the protection of her Lord Jesus to cover them all, no matter how scattered they may be. True to form, she also asked the Lord for forgiveness for the thought of damning any human being, even though it felt like they deserved it. That was God's job, she was taught, no matter how hard it was to leave it that way.

She went to sleep with her bible in her hand and her husband on her heart, wondering how long it would be before she would hear his voice again and if it would be because he was protecting her or because he had gone adrift again.

****

She awoke the next day focused on making the kids as comfortable as possible, no matter how uncomfortable she might be herself, and with pure intention to outdo the norm to which they had become accustomed.

While they all ate their cereal and Buddy watched cartoons, she suggested cheerfully, "What d'ya say we make this place a little nicer?"

April perked up. "What do ya mean, Mama?"

"Well, I been thinkin'…we should git some new furniture for your rooms. Let each of you pick out y'ur own stuff. Think it's about time now."

April was excited. "You mean I can git stuff I like, my own stuff?"

"Sure, baby, "Kathleen said, looking at Jo. "How 'bout you?"

Jo shrugged, slopped her cereal around, and looked at her mom. "Yeah, I guess, whatever."

Buddy ran up to the table. "Mama, can I git stuff too? Boy stuff?"

Kathleen laughed, "Buddy, since when have you not had boy stuff?"

Buddy looked at his feet. "I just thought maybe since Daddy left for milk, they were gonna dress me up like a girl ag'in."

Everyone laughed, albeit half-heartedly, at the memory of Jo and April giving Buddy a full princess make-over, lipstick and all. Billy had lost his mind, of course, but it had lit up the house with laughter like nothing else.

"Well…we will go do that today then. Anything ya

33

want, for your rooms," she said matter-of-factly. "And we best be gettin' some school clothes too, y'all ain't got too much longer 'fore school starts back, and every one of ya are sproutin' like weeds!"

Jo perked up. She loved dressing up and had even started to tinker with make-up here and there. She was excited at the thought of something new to wear and the idea that she would be around more kids her age again. Being out of the house helped her keep moving. But she wasn't much for showing gratitude towards Kathleen in those days. "'Bout time, Mama," was all she said, straight-faced.

Kathleen ignored the slight, pushing the wound back with all the others, and focused on the knowledge that Jo would enjoy this day, even if she wasn't willing to show it. It would be hard for Jo to keep it all inside when Kathleen took her to the make-up counter, like she planned. She would teach her how to wear it, when to wear it, and April would be soon to follow. Or, at least that is how Kathleen saw it going for the girls in her mind.

They got dressed quickly, stopped at the bank to empty an almost drained savings account, and took to Sky City, a local department store nearby where Kathleen would purposefully allow them to run amok, within reason, and entertain anything their little hearts desired. Kathleen let each of the kids pick out everything they wanted to decorate their rooms, so long as it had a function. It made her happy to watch them make their own choices, have their own tastes with a little bit of light in their eyes from both the newness of the items and the normality of shopping. Kathleen even bought a few items for the rest of the house to make it feel happier—a floral print throw for the couch, a couple of candles, and a brightly colored welcome mat for the front door in case anyone came knocking. They were not hoping for just anyone, of course. *Anything to quell the sting.*

Even though Billy was gone, Kathleen made sure the kids knew they had a lot to be thankful for and they should say their thanks accordingly. Kathleen worried that, even though she would teach her children right from wrong morally and biblically, they would have no true life experience or skills to apply that knowledge. In fact, their world would show them the opposite, and for those thoughts and fears, she was angry with Billy.

April and Buddy took to prayer easy. Jo, as always, was a tougher sell when it came to saying, "Thanks a lot," to God. Her daddy had just left her. She was as thick headed and as near-sighted as he always had been, and she had a keen eye, focused on the leaves…not even the trees, much less the entire forest.

"I know why we got to go git all them things, Mama. I ain't dumb," Jo said to her mom in front of April as they climbed into their beds.

"What do ya mean, JoAnne?" Kathleen asked.

Jo didn't like it when either of her parents used her proper first name. "Ya know what I mean. Just 'cuz Daddy ain't here. This stuff don't make me feel no better. 'Sides, how ya plannin' on payin' bills now that ya done got us all this *stuff*?" She had said the word like it was filth on her tongue.

Kathleen leaned against the wall, hiding her heartbreak as best as she could. "I got ya this *stuff* because I thought ya might like it. If ya don't, I can surely take it back. And bills ain't y'ur concern."

"Yeah, they're Daddy's, and he ain't here, so they're y'urs now. Ain't that how that works? Guess ya best find ya a new man to pay our bills," she said, turning her back to Kathleen as she pulled her new comforter up to her chin.

"JoAnne Darcy Pierce, I will not have ya talkin'

to me like that. Ya best think about apologizin', either to me or to the Lord. I don't care which…but he does." She switched off the light and left the room without hesitation.

She heard April admonishing Jo as she walked the hall to her bedroom, but she let it go. Resuming church attendance would now be on the weekly agenda, she resolved.

Besides the ordinary ruckus that consistently ensued between the girls who shared a room, but not an ounce of personality, and the growing sharpness of Jo's resentment of her entire life situation, the day they got to shop for whatever they wanted was about as excited as the new family unit would get for a while. Kathleen was overwhelmed, but she still noticed the slow drive-bys that came down the road and around the bend on the regular. Although they didn't voice it to one another, they all secretly waited for the phone to ring, to hear his voice, or even less likely, the door to swing open to their daddy's white t-shirt, blue jeans, and work boots.

CHAPTER EIGHT

When Billy woke up in the back of the bar, he was in a different world. The others were still there. They had waited on him, maybe caught some sleep themselves, but they had been talking and decided they wanted Billy to join them on their ride to Jacksonville. That was where they were ultimately headed, they said, and he couldn't remember if they had discussed it before or if it just sounded familiar because maybe, somewhere along the line, he had thought it. He had thought so much, he had confused himself. Troll, of course, didn't quite agree that Billy should follow, much less join them in anything. *Shitstick*. That, he remembered for sure. It didn't bother him, though. Troll was nothing to Billy. He had met and known many nothings, and he had just left everything. "Just," being a relative term, of course.

Billy had no solid plans, and Jacksonville seemed as good as any. Not too far. He could keep an ear out for any possible news from back home. He meant to call Kathleen already. He just didn't know what to say, and he didn't know who was listening. Their safety was his main concern, and until he secured that for the long term, he wouldn't risk it for a brief delight for either of them.

The sun hit him hard. "Hooo-ly Shit!" he said with one hand over his eyes as Hatchett threw the metal door open in demonstrative fashion like he was opening the door to life itself.

"Yes sir! That there is a right Florida day's sunshine!"

"Damn, Hatchett, you are one perky son a bitch," Henry-Nine said, lighting up a smoke.

Hatchett smiled. "You know it."

"Maybe we should have called you…Smiley," Niner retorted as they went to shoving and wrestling in the parking lot.

"I'll smile as I piss on your knocked-out ass!"

Billy liked their style but had more interest in the bikes than the grappling show. He made his way over to where they were parked, lined up in diagonal fashion, like they belonged on a kick-line. He looked them over. Most he recognized—Harleys—one and all.

"Tell me 'bout this one on the end."

"The one on the end. You hear that, assholes? He wants to know about the one on the end," Hatchett said, hurrying over.

Billy could tell he was proud. "Don't git too damn excited. I just don't recognize a few parts is all," he said, eager to get in on the jawin'. "Ya like a little girl or sumthin'."

Niner laughed. It took a minute, but Hatchett did too. Troll lingered against the dirty building.

The others were clearly surplus scoots-Harleys to be sure, but somewhere along the line, the Outlanders had picked them up at bargain price and chopped off the rifle-scabbards and radio-mounts that the bikes once required for their military use. Choppers, by their very definition.

It was clear they all had an affinity for Harley. Maybe it was the brand's hard edge and the lure of freedom and escape. But Hatchett's bike was no surplus. "I like it. I done rode me some bikes, but nuthin' like this one." It looked brand new…and expensive.

"She is fresh. Harley FXWG, Wide Glide 80ci," Hatchett crooned with pride.

Billy touched her smooth lines, and even through the oil and dust, he fell in love with her. "She is sumthin, a'ight."

Hatchett and Niner looked at one another. "It's going to take me a minute to get used to that accent, for sure! We will get you on a bike when we get where we are going. You owe us a dirt show. That car is a sweetheart. I bet you could turn her loose pretty good, huh?"

Billy looked back at his car, almost forgetting. She was new to him, and he hadn't pushed her full on, but he was sure he could impress anyone in any car he was driving, had he the need or desire. And he always had *that* desire. *Fast cars and fast women… and fast bikes*? He thought, for sure, the minute he got to riding with the big boys, it would make the shortlist. And he always wanted what he wanted, and until this point, he had wanted to turn around and go home to his wife and kids, which wasn't a possibility.

Following as they flew their colors, he trailed them to Jacksonville, occasionally passing and flipping them off if he felt they were moving a little too slow for his liking. He eased in line behind them as they rolled into town and slowed up into the parking lot of "Night Moves," a strip club that boasted "Jacksonville's Finest and Fanciest Ladies" on its signage. Entering the dark bar, surrounded by loud, long-hair music, half-dressed ladies, and men of every variety and persuasion, Billy thought to himself, *If these are the finest and fanciest ladies in Jacksonville, then I'm in the wrong place.* Hatchett led the group to the back booth and pushed up into a round alcove complete with heavy, draped, red velvet curtains that could be closed, should the need arise. A topless, young African American woman saddled in next to Hatchett.

"Haven't seen you in a while, sugar," she said to him, clearly familiar.

Hatchett took one of her hands and kissed it. "I've been working doll-face. Now, be a love and go fetch us some whiskey."

She obliged easily. This wasn't the kind of place a woman got offended by being asked kindly to do anything. As she walked across the room to the bar, Hatchett watched her backside. "Ahhhh, Miss Destiny Rhodes. Just as good from the back as she is up front. Don't you think?"

Billy looked her over once more. "She's a'ight. Ain't no Georgia peach though."

"Georgia peach? Wild loves him some peaches, boys. Peaches juicier in Georgia?" he teased.

Billy thought on it. "Gimme a li'l bit, and I'll tell ya."

They all went to howling at his response, even Troll. "Well, there's a first," Hatchett said in Troll's direction. And Troll immediately sturdied his face as the drinks were placed on the table by the topless looker. "Thank you, gorgeous," Hatchett said, placing a twenty on the tray. She smiled and blew him a kiss as she took the tray and turned to leave. They were calling her name to the stage. In no time at all, the men were silently watching Destiny perform and writhe to the steady tune and tone of the Eagles crooning about "Those Shoes." Her dance garnered high praise and double-fingered whistles. It was fitting. She was a sure and slow sexy show, right down to those clear, platform shoes.

They took to drinking again, but this time, the talk was serious and steady. There weren't any jokes or digs. Nobody interrupted anybody. And the naked girls dancing—it was as though they weren't even there, except for the greetings that each one would voice to the table as they passed by. Billy was keenly aware that he was with regulars. Respected regulars at that.

Hatchett would fill him in on the club. Non-proprietary information of course, but tons of it. The others would add details or ask questions when they felt it necessary, but always in turn.

Although he had heard stories and random pieces of information in his years of making the shine runs, only then did he recognize the Outlanders as a serious motorcycle club—one that would conduct itself publicly in a highly professional manner. He realized, now, that they wouldn't go out of their way to cause trouble or present themselves as an intimidating force without purpose or provocation. Their respect was gained from that, he realized, remembering the way he had carried on with Hatchett, Henry-Nine, and even Troll back in Jasper.

Billy relayed his intentions to get a steady job, to

provide for his wife and kids, and to make it on his own terms. He would hole up in a small motel room in town until he could make enough money to get his own place and his own bike—his new goals. If he was going to be far from home, or just far enough, he wanted to make a life. Even if he intended it to be a relatively brief stay, he would make it his. He wanted to feel connected, and the men he had met were just those type of men, luckily. He ran across an ad in the local paper for a marble installer, and he was on the phone in a flash.

"Do you have experience?" was all they really asked, and he rattled off the years of time he had spent on marble, framing, carpentry, and every other aspect of any job they might need looked after or taken care of, and he was hired instantly—sight unseen. It would keep his bills paid and his days full, if nothing else. And he knew he would need work outside the interests of the Club, save a favor or two, even though Hatchett had made the offer. He wanted friends, not potential enemies, and he had already made them in Hatchett and Henry-Nine. He didn't want to patch in or make any official commitments, and they knew it. He just wasn't that type of guy, either personally or pro- fessionally. Never had been.

But he couldn't escape the truth, and truth be told, although Billy's first passion was for cars, maybe because he had been around them his entire life, he definitely had an interest in bikes. *Going fast.* They had that in common— Billy, the cars, and the bikes. In 1953, the granddaddy of all outlaw biker flicks had been released: "The Wild One," starring Marlon Brando, and once Billy had seen it later in life, he had never forgotten it, nor had most boys who were lured into the roar of the road by the big screen version. The story about bikers, their immoral morals, mirrored their own dreams and demons. Like so many others, Billy had loved Brando's sneering face, his leather, his attitude. He even recognized himself in the name. He was *Wild*, after all.

Billy would become a motorcycle man within a month of starting his day job, and his first love would be a 1957 black and silver, rigid-frame, Harley shovelhead that Hatchett had "found" for Billy. It didn't come without a price, though.

"Time to pay up."

Billy pulled his wallet from his pocket. "How much I owe ya?"

Hatchett smacked the wallet away with the back of his hand. "I don't want your money, Billy boy. I want your blood."

For a moment, Billy was taken aback. "Say ag'in?"

"Time for some ink," Hatchett said.

Billy relaxed. "Hmm. A'ight. Let's do it."

Within the next few hours, he had the clean tattoo of an eagle with its wings spread open on his forearm, and he was ready to soar.

CHAPTER NINE

Through Hatchett, Billy was introduced to a host of clubbers, from prospects to a fine, old grey-beard they called "Ghost". Story was he could get you anything from anywhere, and nobody would ever know how he got it or where it came from. Billy believed every word because damn if that old man wouldn't show up right next to him without so much as a hint of a whisper and scare the ever-loving shit out of him every time.

There was a long list of requirements for joining the Outlanders, and Billy was not surprised to learn that the list included owning a functioning Harley-Davidson. Rare exceptions, such as Indians and Buells, were occasionally permitted, and in which case, both the bike and the person were considered prospects. In addition to just owning a bike, members were expected to utilize the V-twin-powered Harleys as their primary means of transportation. Not many prospects ever took issue with this rule.

So many of the men Billy met were Vietnam veterans, lost to society by most accounts. Disenfranchised or not, most of those returning soldiers felt strongly about the country they fought for. With this sense of loyalty, identity, and true patriotism, most of the veterans Billy met by way of Hatchett's introductions wouldn't have even considered buying a non-US-made motorcycle. So for the Outlanders, Harley Davidson reigned supreme.

Although they seemed to treat him like a probate, not quite a prospect, Billy came to be known and respected as one of the first, straight-up, no bullshit, no hassles "Free Riders", men who shared the same values and enjoyed the same lifestyle as the Outlanders but preferred to keep a degree of freedom of choice by not formally belonging to the club. Billy became an exception to the rule, where there were no exceptions. It felt similar in kind to how he treated Dixie and company back home. That hadn't gone unnoticed or unchecked, of course. After all, clubs like the Outlanders drew members that they deemed worthy. People didn't typically hunt them down for membership. Instead, they found their affiliates in those who needed the road perhaps slightly less than the road needed them. But Billy had known people that their people knew, and he checked out well as a probate. Better than most, actually. They were familiar with the Dixie Mafia, and they became familiar with its members on purpose and in the course of verifying Billy's identity and credibility. Billy's stories about who he was checked out. He was there by choice, that much was certain, but he wouldn't be prospecting, fetching anyone's anything, responding with any "how highs", or cleaning any bikes or bitches for members.

Hatchett found the information he gleaned from Billy's hometown interesting. And he was specifically enthralled with the lore of the Dixie Mafia. He honed-in on their goals and endeavors, realizing that what made the Outlanders different from the Dixie Mafia was that crime and violence were not used as expedients in pursuit of any profits. Their specific priorities were, in fact, reversed completely. Mayhem and lawlessness were inherent in living "Outlander life," but the profits, possessions, or money they obtained by illegal means was only wanted as a way to perpetuate that lifestyle. Hatchett appreciated their way of doing things and wondered how Billy felt about it, now having been around both.

Armed with the knowledge of Billy's past, Hatchett knew and had told the others that Billy, being part of that lifestyle, although a Free Rider, would be particularly happy to participate in whatever they asked of him, and to that end, he would be a great ally. As a bonus, his talents and participation would likely yield lucrative. Billy was fully aware of what was going on around him. It wasn't atypical in Night Moves to see piles of weed and cocaine on the table while the bikies smoked and purchased pounds from the runners.

Some nights, Hatchett would mention it. "You up for a run, Billy boy?"

Billy would nod in agreement, stoic and unfazed. "Say when."

Hatchett would pat him on the back and go about his business, mostly drinking and occasionally drugging. He seemed to stay away from the strippers though, unlike most of his cohorts. "I'm not too keen on sharing," he would say. He was looking for an ol' lady, Billy knew. But the lifestyle didn't exactly shoot the clean ones straight through the system on a golden, virginal platter. So, Hatchett indulged here and there, but never openly.

Although it seemed they spent most of their time

and talk in the strip club, Billy came to learn that the Out-landers had acquired an old building on the outskirts for use as their official clubhouse. They called it "church". For the longest time, he thought they might be a religious bunch the way they were always headed for church. But this was no cathedral, no heavenly sanctuary of grace and goodness. They had installed barbed-wire topped fences around the sacred building, and the walls were reinforced with plate steel. It wasn't exactly divine or spiritual, aesthetically speaking.

****

It was late afternoon, when Billy had surpassed a construction deadline by well over a week, that Hatchett had called Billy to the carpet for driving the Rambler to the bar. On most days, Billy would park the four wheels at home and swap them for two.

"Shit, I just came from work."

Hatchett grabbed his arm before he could take a sip of the cold beer he had been looking forward to all day long. "It's time I see why you love those things so much. I just flat don't believe you drive like you say you can drive." It was a dare, designed to incite Billy. And it worked.

As he had promised long before, Billy followed Hatchett and Henry-Nine out to a deserted lot, which seemed to have been a small shopping mall at one point but now boasted nothing in the way of wares. They dismount-ed their bikes and stood in silence, waiting for Billy to do something.

"The fuck is he doing?" Niner asked.

"Looks like he is fooling with the radio?"

In fact, that was exactly what Billy was doing. Finding his muse, as he had so often when he really wanted to turn her loose. He heard it when he crossed it on the dial. "That'll do," he mumbled to himself.

Looking over at the men, he roared the engine as a teaser. Hatchett yelled, "C'mon now Wild. Show us something!"

And he let her rip to the not-so-subtle subtle soundtrack of Eddie Rabbitt singing "Driving My Life Away". The tires spun, and the rubber wailed as he laid into the concrete like the ass end of the car was on fire. He pegged her as fast as she could be pegged and drifted into a turn where the concrete ended, squaring her back up. He weaved her to and fro, through the concrete posts, swinging her back end around at each asphalt dryline. And then for fun, he swung her hard left, leaning in, and then hard right, leaning in, same as he had the night in the church parking lot. This figure eight wasn't smothered in pain, it was drowning in pride. He kept on for what seemed an eternity, a genuine and remembered rush, until the smoke was thick and the rubber felt like it might not hold out. For punctuation, he parked her in one clean spin just in front of their feet. And he meant to. Or they would be dead.

"Ho-ly shit!" Hatchett wailed. "I mean damn!"

Billy climbed out of the car and leaned up against her, seeming cool as a cucumber and lit up a smoke. "That work?"

Niner reached out his hand, and Billy took it, shaking it firm. "That there was a show, boy. You weren't lying. You are a driver. I'll take that bet any day."

"Me too. That was wild…WILD!" Hatchett shook his hand too. "My man, showing class," Hatchett hollered to nobody in particular. Billy knew by now what he meant. He had been immersed and around the Club long enough to understand their lingo. Hatchett had just paid him a compliment most wouldn't understand, but Billy took to heart. *Showing class*, he thought. *Ain't that cool?* He had performed an act a "citizen", or non-motorcyclist, wouldn't or couldn't do. He guessed it worked for cars too, at least in this case.

They were just as pleased with him as he was with himself. So it was time.

Hatchett looked at Niner and nodded. "We're going to need to do some business with you at your house to-night."

Billy obliged, "That's fine. Think y'all can keep up?"

"Funny fucker," Niner answered as they mounted their bikes.

Back at Billy's, Hatchett dished the deal. Billy would make a run for the good stuff, the stuff that was exploding everywhere. He'd head down to Daytona Beach to retrieve the goods. They would take care of payment. Billy was just the pick-up and delivery man. They only dealt with one man in particular, because they trusted him and they trusted his product, knowing that once cocaine hit the street, it was often cut with a bunch of agents to buff it out, giving shady dealers a bigger profit. They wouldn't be having that. And Billy wasn't to stray the line either. They would pay double, or even triple, the regular price for the cleanest and purest there was. Once he had the goods in sight, made nice with the seller, and secured the load, it was back to Jacksonville. He wouldn't ask any questions of anybody. He would keep it simple and covert. There was to be no exchanging of names or pleasantries. He would tell work he was taking a vacation, and when he got back, he wouldn't talk to or see anyone, especially any Outlanders, for a week or so. He would drive his own car, and if it all went well, they would reward him handsomely. With what, he didn't ask. He didn't have to. The thought of it brought back the rush, just as he had skinned the wheels on the pavement just a few hours before.

"I'm in."

Hatchett and Niner shoved off the table, and each gave him a pat him on the back in turn as they left. "Let us know when you plan to leave work."

"I'll be leavin' work tomorrow, boys. Ain't that the deal?"

Hatchett leaned back in the house. "Right man for the job. Knew you were. *Always* knew."

Billy found it hard to sleep, thinking on the drive and the drugs. Those rocket shots of adrenaline he used to chase were now chasing him again. He didn't know how or when he would know where he was headed, but he didn't concern himself with those details. They would be taken care of, no doubt. And when he rose in the morning, there was a small piece of paper in his coffee pot with a Daytona Beach address on it. He hadn't noticed Hatchett or Niner go anywhere near the counter the night before, and he realized it was entirely possible someone had slipped in and out while he was drifting in and out of sleep. *Ghost*, he was sure of it. *Sneaky old fucker.* He must have been some kind of dangerous when he was a young man. Billy made mental note to spend some quality time with the grey-beard when he got back. He knew he had a few good stories to tell if, in fact, he could or would tell them. Billy would offer a few of his own in fair trade.

The crazy abilities of Ghost would be but one of the many things Billy would think about as he drove down to the beach. He cruised easy, enjoying the drive and the solitude, something that wasn't generally his thing. He thought about Kathleen and the kids, wondered what they were doing and if they had grown used to his absence or mourned him as though he were dead. It was enough to make him even more homesick than crazy, and on a lone-some highway, he spotted a phone booth. He succumbed to a rare moment of weakness and called his wife, but there was no answer. Not that he had intended on telling her anything of consequence, he just missed the sound of her voice and wanted to assure her that she and the kids were on his mind all the time. Just in case they doubted his love and need for them, he wanted to get out a few solid "I miss you and love you-s". Realistically, he kept them off his mind as much as possible, but only to ease the pain of their absence. He thought that was fair, but he didn't want them doing the same, of course. Back in the car, he grew thank-ful he wasn't driving and crying based on a conversation he could have had with his estranged family. That's what they were now, he figured—strangers. People he had literally left in the dust, not entirely by his own choosing. He hated the thought of it.

Shifting gears, he sped her up and at the same time, shifted mental gears to the task at hand. He had been asked to sample the merchandise before returning with it, lest he bring a trunk-load of dirt. And they had thrown out a line for him to sample so he would know what feeling he was looking for *exactly*. Hesitant at first but feeling the pull of the roulette game he had played with Dixie around a simi-lar table, in a similar dining room, not so very long ago, he grabbed the rolled-up bill from Hatchett's hand and pulled the trigger. *What a rush.* Hatchett and Niner followed with straight cuts, but only the bare minimum.

"Don't you go getting attached to this high. It isn't worth it," Hatchett warned. "You stay cranked up like this for too long, you won't have enough sense to get out of the shower to shit."

He noticed everybody called it something different, and the few times he tried it, just for posterity, he figured out why. Mostly, it seemed like the potency or the pureness of the drug prompted the long list of monikers by which the users would refer to it. It was a hell of a drug, Billy learned quickly, and it could mess a person up real quick, in all ways, if they let it. In the few hours he spent between the hotel pool and the room where the deal actually went down, the Florida snow was everywhere, in every shape and form. It was the first and only time he saw anyone free-base the cola. He noticed it took less product for the smokers to gain faster and seemingly more intense results. *Can't be good*, he thought.

Billy eased the Rambler into a parking spot, backside in, up against the pool area, as instructed and watched through shaded lenses from a poolside lounger as the man placed the previously inspected and tested contents of four suitcases into her trunk. Billy noticed he moved easy and appeared as though he was nothing more than a traveler loading up his personals to hit the road after a long vacation. This definitely wasn't *his* first rodeo.

As instructed in the hotel room, Billy took his time by the pool, even jumping in to cool off and slugging back a beer another sun-lover had offered him, before throwing his shirt on and hitting the road. When he was back on the highway, he was keenly aware of the contents of his trunk, just like he had been the first time he ran shine, before he got back to being himself—cocky, looking to toy with the law like he did so many times in those days with a loaded trunk. *This is more serious than a few jugs of firewater*, he had to tell himself a few times when he got the itch to put more weight on the pedal. He managed to move her just the way all the others on the same stretch did and made it into his driveway. He felt good, high on the thrill of success. All he had to do was wait. For what, he didn't know.

He was growing bored of waiting. Sitting around in one place, any place, even his home, was never his strong suit. Just as he planned to hit the local liquor store, he heard the purr of Hatchett's bike on his street. *Thank the Lord*, he thought to himself. And then he rethought what he had just said in his mind. And it made him uncomfortable. None of this was the Lord's work, he knew. He could hear Kathleen's prayers, and they wouldn't stop until Hatchett was praising him on a job well done and insisting they tow the white line together, for fun. Just this one time.

"Take your car and follow me," Hatchett insisted.

"My car? I was plannin' on ridin' tonight."

Hatchett laughed as though Billy had just told a joke, and Billy got the feeling it was a joke. An inside joke he wasn't a part of. "You will."

Billy trailed Hatchett to the old junkyard outside town where the others seemed to have been for hours by the looks of things. Most of them half-drunk, raising hell in all sorts of ways. This wasn't the kind of function Billy had normally been invited to or part of with Hatchett before. Hatchett saw the look on Billy's face. "Ahhh don't worry. You're clear." He leaned into Billy's car and grabbed the keys, heading for the trunk. "And it's *clean*."

Niner tossed Billy an ice-cold beer the minute he got out of the car, which was followed by a series of pats on the back and varying words of approval.

"Nice job," one man mumbled, leaning in close to Billy's left ear. The lingering haze of whiskey's hum snaked through his lips.

"Fuuuuck yeah!" another slurred.

He felt like he was one of them, and for just a moment, he wanted to be.

"Bring it around men!" Hatchett yelled to the crowd.

Everyone slowly made their way to Hatchett, having emptied Billy's trunk. Billy thought he saw Hatchett put something into the trunk as well, just as he was standing strong and proud of his go-to guy, the man who wasn't a brother but had treated them well and as promised. "Billy here has delivered and delivered big, my brothers. What do you say we celebrate…accordingly?" he said, nodding at Niner.

On cue, Niner flipped his zippo and tossed it into the empty trunk. And the fire lit loose on the Rambler. Billy instinctively lunged forward, but Hatchett caught him. "Let her go. It's alright."

Watching the car go up, listening to everyone go crazy at the sight, Billy got a strange sense of foreboding he could not identify. He brushed it off, bringing himself back to the moment and the realization that he no longer had a car. Damnit if he didn't wish he had Coop right down the road to fix that problem as he had so many times in the past. He would have to swing by Coop's place if he got to run to Georgia, he thought, to check his inventory. But he wasn't sure he wanted to run to Georgia. Or even run again. No matter that now, because that was putting the cart before the horse. And right this very minute, the cart was on fire.

"Your ride is over there," Hatchett said, nodding towards the bike Hatchett had given him. "I don't have to tell you…Ghost brought her. She is your number one girl now. You stay on two wheels."

Billy felt an allegiance and a duty to honor that request. If he were to stay.

CHAPTER TEN

He used to tear it up. Back before he was the "go-to" guy, the "what say you" man, the barely older, yet somehow decades wiser, dealer of dirt and dust.

Coop went to rip-roaring, something that had been happening with more and more frequency lately. He'd wake himself up at about four in the morning, fix himself a pot of coffee, drink the whole damn thing, and then be on the shine by eight, watching the heat cook up an early fall's southern swelter.

Something in the shine made him angry. Hell, life made him angry. There was barely anyone around anymore to shoot the shit with, and that burned him up in a way the in-between season's cooker never could.

It was like they all forgot about him. Or, at least he felt like they did. Used him for what he had and tossed him aside. He hated the thoughts and the pains that came with age. He hated everything these days, and it showed on his face, ten times worse for the wear.

Donna was the unfortunate brunt of the end of those moonshine days, though she knew better than to hang around and simply wait for it. She never had been one to chime in or present herself for show unless Coop asked anyway. He had always been her keeper, and she was in it for the long haul. But he had grown odd, even by her standards, in recent days, and she stayed clear of him best she could. Until she couldn't. Because she never even saw it coming. Same as him.

She hadn't done much to provoke him that night. She gave up reasoning or even conversing with him long ago. *She didn't feel or know a thing*, of that he thought he was sure. *She never did*, actually. Like a thorn that unrelentingly torments you with its presence but never bothers itself, it's just doing what thorns do. *Same as her*, he soothed himself, and by the next morning, he thought he didn't feel or know a thing either. He was wrong. At first, he had graphic and raging flashes, but the day's shine dimmed those to tiny little floaters, the sparkly erratic dots a person might get if they were upside down or holding their breath too long. Until he passed out on the porch swing watching traffic go by, wanting and waiting for someone, anyone, to stop by. He would have given anything to do some wheeling and dealing, of any kind.

It wasn't like he had never done anything bad in his life before. In reality, he had been breaking the law since he was a teenager and even stole a pack of tobacco or two before that. But murder wasn't exactly stealing tobacco now, was it? *Was that what it was*?

Oh, he had taken a life a time or two, albeit nonhuman, and truth be told, he didn't feel too much about that at all. Most bad things can be explained away by blaming away, and that is what most folks Coop knew did. *Do, blame, block, repeat.* Simpletons in a simple place making simple decisions on basic impulse.

The small flashbulbs in the recesses of his brain grew into a spotlight on a grandiose stage, and there they were. Just a good stretch away from the house, Coop and Donna were putting on a play in the theatre of his mind, and it was certainly a crowd stunner. Like at the movie house when something horrible happened on the screen and nobody watching knew how to react. Coop remembered a time that had happened and thought it unnerving that, in a room full of people, you could hear someone swallow if you listened hard enough.

The old well was a shadow in the backdrop, and Coop was carrying Donna over his shoulder like a rag doll, his own labored breathing deep amidst the crickets and crunch of scorched weeds. And then, his mind reversed itself and the playhouse. "He" was walking backwards, the same way he had come, all the way up to the house and into the kitchen where he took Donna from his shoulder and laid her on the laminate floor next to a large cast iron skillet. He placed her head in a pool of fresh blood, her house dress splayed around her like a ball gown. He got up slow, hand on one knee, and looked down at her as the skillet jumped into his hand. She rose in one swift, yet limp motion from the floor. As Coop turned back to the cooktop, he grazed the crown of her head with the cast iron. And Donna went to washing dishes behind him.

CHAPTER ELEVEN

The concrete edges were rough but suitable for their purpose. Grey and weathered, scraps of solid cinder stones stacked in round rows about waist high, the weeds around which were equally statured. Just a simple circle in the back forty that had seen its share of secrets and outlived its intended purpose years ago. Many an animal and lye had known its depths, but of the rest, Coop wasn't sure. He had heard stories, same as everyone else, but even though it stood firm on his property, he left it alone. He knew when to put up, and he had always known when to shut up. It wasn't much for ornament, but it certainly decorated the minds of anyone who was dumb enough or unlucky enough to ask about it or have it shown to them. A simple well…with immense depth. And not a soul around to give a care to what may or may not be at the bottom, if it wasn't, in fact, bottomless.

CHAPTER TWELVE

"I know he came to you, ol' man," Dixie said in no uncertain, declarative terms.

Coop shoved his hands into his signature overalls, chewed a bit harder, scrunched his cheeks, and spat near Dixie's feet...almost.

"He always comes to me. That ain't no thang."

Dixie huffed, almost a laugh, looked Coop up and down, and started towards the creek. "What say ya come on down here and take a listen?"

Coop grew uneasy. It was a welling in his denim belly he had not felt in quite some time. Maybe because most times he wasn't here nor there thanks to the shine.

"Yeah. A'ight."

Dixie trekked through the trees of Coop's property, crunching his way over scorched grass and bur whistles as Coop followed him down. They both knew where they were ultimately headed. Dixie started to whistle. An old tune. Not one anyone but the boys from those parts would know, of course, but one that resonated. Billie Holiday's "Southern Trees". He even mumbled a few lyrics. "Southern trees have strange fruit, blood on the leaves and some on the root." He looked back at Coop, trailing a calculated distance behind.

"That's enough now, Dixie. What d'ya want from me," Coop asked, feeling winded from the walk and the sparkling from the damn floaters.

"Just a lil' bit more," Dixie said as he rounded the huge Magnolia tree. "Ahhh, now *there* is a good restin' place."

Coop knew. And he knew that Dixie knew too. Of course, he knew. There wasn't a person in the world that Coop would ever tell, but Dixie knew in his black soul when he heard she was gone. It gave him the juice that would coarse through his veins and reinvigorate the beating of his heart.

Dixie sat on the ledge of the well, lifted his head a bit as if he was taking in the wind, save there was no wind. "Hmmm...sumthin' smells...off 'round here."

Coop stirred uneasy, hands still in his pockets, churning and chewing the tobacco in his cheek.

Dixie pulled a smoke from his pocket, lit her easy, and leaned back over the well, blowing his first drag into the air. He raised his hands as if to mimic a dance of the smoke over the well. His signature twitch of a smirk catching the curl of the corners of his mouth. "You know what

I'm askin' ya, Coop. Ain't nothin' else I want. What did ya give him, and where did he go?"

"C'mon now, Dixie," Coop pleaded in the mildest version imaginable. "Ya know I do business 'round here too. Can't go tellin' everyone e'rythang." He knew it was a fruitless venture to skirt any questions or demands from this man, but he would draw it out, so long as he could stay alive in the interim, on principle alone.

Dixie pulled hard on his cigarette, turning to look at Coop, a good ten feet away. "Why don't ya come on over here, throw ya a penny down the well. Maybe y'ur wishes will come true, Coop."

"I git it, Dixie. I git it. He come over here needin' to leave town on account of ya sayin' he did. I sold him a car, and he left. Wasn't nothin' more to it than that."

Dixie laughed. "Wasn't there?" He paused, looked at Coop, leaned back over the well as if he was glaring into its dark secrets, then back to Coop again. "What kind of car? *I'll leave ya there then.*"

"That's all I know, and I ain't tryin' to keep it from ya neither...a Rambler."

Dixie stood up, smiling from ear to ear, and fingered Coop over to the edge of the well. Coop walked slowly toward him, obliging. "What color?"

Coop looked at his feet. "Oh, ya know, that green-ish, maybe silver color."

Dixie cleared his throat. "Say a'gin? What *color*?" He emphasized the last word, not keen to Coop making him repeat himself.

"Green," was all Coop could say.

"Thanks, Coop. That's all I wanted. What ya so

scared of anyway?" Dixie questioned as he grabbed onto Coop's overall strap, took his last drag, and tossed his cigarette down the well.

He yanked the strap forward and past his own body towards the deep hole as he walked away and looked over his shoulder as Coop fell onto the edge of the concrete, watching the cigarette fall.

Dixie grew happy as a shithouse rat at the sight of the shame and the stitch he had just created.

CHAPTER THIRTEEN

Back in 1972, when Governor Jimmy Carter commissioned a task force to establish a master plan to implement a Criminal Justice Information System for Georgia, Dixie and crew were already on the way to certain ruin, but nobody really knew it. Criminal activity of all types was increasing dramatically across the state, and Governor Carter was convinced that more timely and accurate crime information would be extremely beneficial to state and local law enforcement agencies, especially the small-towners where shit went down without word or penalty.

The Georgia Bureau of Investigation had the responsibility of maintaining criminal identification records, and that became the focal point in Georgia. The collection, storage, rapid retrieval, and dissemination of law enforcement, and criminal justice related information quickly put Winder, Georgia on the map. They saw everything Watts and his men saw, did…and didn't do. They had more questions than answers, and that drew them in.

In the Bureau's "war-room", they had been watching for quite some time. James Bates, or "Dixie", as the others would call him, had shown up as a blip on their radar screen some years ago, and then, swiftly, he became the Hindenburg. This once loosely woven tapestry of small syndicates had multiplied, intermingled, and spread somewhat like wildfire right under their noses. Typically not drawn to the small town, back door dealings of the outskirts, the Bureau couldn't help but notice the growing number of criminal ideations and the link to almost every single one of them—James Bates. He was everywhere, and yet, he was nowhere. Yes, they had heard about him. Yes, he had been implicated by more than one of his acquaintances, but that is all they were. "Met him once" or "might know him" kind of guys. A name drop by people here and there who had tripped up of their own accord, and it was always the same. They couldn't prove who knew him or who didn't. Yet.

Dixie thought the law had their eyes on him, maybe not keenly, but with his circle of knowledge growing ever greater, more and more of the men he knew, used and dealt with, mostly outside of town, were making mistakes and ending up in the slammer. He had heard it once or twice. "The law is comin' down on the Dixie Mafia" over in Birmingham, or anywhere but where he was, and he knew it was only a matter of time before they tried to hit the small towns just the same. But he was smarter than most, he always believed, and he didn't intend on being tied to anyone who had anything to do with anything. If he did, they knew the consequence. They would "forget" they even knew him, one way or the other.

Besides, he always said, "I ain't part of no gang or

nothin' like that. I don't need that shit. I'm my own man, and I'm man enough." He knew full well what and who he was dealing with and, for the most part, that he was in charge of it all in his part of the world and even reaching further. By the time Billy Pierce left town, Dixie was respected and feared in at least three states, best he could figure. And whether they had feelings about him or not, the rest of Dixieland had heard of him.

Ain't no law can measure what I done here and there. And if any others would talk, bein' scared of me don't break the law, he resolved.

And that kept him just out of reach of the local law and Officer Watts, who'd been on his case for some time since Billy "up and left". Dixie couldn't quite figure why Watts had such interest in Billy's leavin', but he wasn't the only one, and that made Dixie about as nervous as he was capable of becoming. Which was just a hair shy of not at all. He would see them coming, he thought, were they to come for him. After all, he *ain't never done nothin' wrong*. Or so his story would go. And he believed that story with the entirety of anything he had in him, which wasn't much in the way of heart.

As big and untouchable as he was in his own mind, his face hung madly in the middle of their target board. What was once a few smirking mugs had become a full wall of mysteries, an intricate web woven by photos of madmen and arrows. They had nailed a few, but a few only. Law wasn't thick in the rural areas of the South, and as anyone in those parts knew, that's why Dixie and company pulled any string on that web they chose. Mostly, without recourse. Anyone who really knew anything would disappear or clam up. The Bureau watched, of course. Some would even say they "let" it happen. But you can't go chasing ghosts with a badge and a pistol. So the big boys at the Bureau would wait until those ghosts made a rare, human mistake. And on that day, they would have their séance.

It started the way any conjuring would, with a single match. The Gentry farm had gone up in flames, and while they once watched from afar, the big boys came to town for this one. In fact, the day Billy and Dixie were having words on the side of the road, Agent Brightling and Officer Watts were having their own words at Winder's one-stop cop shop. The Bureau would be taking this one over, and even if local police, all six of them, were so inclined, there was nothing they could do about it. It had been too much, the way the local criminals—"Dixie's Mafia" the Bureau would call it—in this town had run wild and free. They had gone too far. Without so much as a question over coffee and donuts. Watts had been taking the hits from higher up for their lack of law management for quite some time, but his resources were slim, and his officers were not exactly *clean*, best he could tell. He didn't figure they were in on anything of much significance, but he was in the wrong, regardless, and he knew it. And now Old Man Gentry had paid the price, along with his entire family. Watts carried the weight of that with him like a ton of bricks linked to a rope hanging around his neck. It would suffocate him eventually, if he let it. And he didn't even know the half of it...the sick, twisted, bloody half of it.

They would start with an old man who went by the name of "Coop" first, though. They didn't want him for anything other than facts and figures. He was a community staple, and just as they knew most of everything they knew without saying, so did he. But he would say, or they would have him...or so they would tell him.

It had come to their attention that his wife had gone missing, or so the rumor mill had churned out, and he hadn't done much about it. Not entirely atypical for these parts. Wives seemed to leave on a whim quite frequently, same as husbands—but usually, they left and took up with the neighbor or a friend of a friend. This one seemed a bit different. Married for twenty-something years, relationship always private, she wasn't known in the community like he was, and he was known to wheel and deal. Not enough for them to care, but most recently, around the time Coop's wife had split, word had it that Dixie had paid Coop a visit. And that was something they couldn't, or wouldn't, let pass.

Maybe one more nail, not that they needed one.

CHAPTER FOURTEEN

Coop was out back wandering around the few cars he had left to sell or tinker with when Brightling showed up. He had taken back up with being outside since Donna was gone. He didn't care too much for the house, kitchen especially, but he didn't wander too far from the immediate yard either. It was almost like he was in prison. Self-made, of course, but he was certainly confined to a designated area, both physically and mentally.

"Hey there. You must be Edward ope," Brightling said, coming around the old truck, seeming to startle the man.

Having never heard his full and rightful name out loud in this town, Coop startled. "Who's askin'?"

Brightling smiled. "I wasn't asking."

Coop took note. His tone, the way he was dressed, his presence. Must be law. "I guess I am. "'Cept, I go by 'Coop'. Always have."

"Yeah, I know." Brightling looked over the truck. "She's nice. Chevy C10. Rare. Two- wheel drive. Short box, 1966. You selling it?"

Coop smirked. "You lookin' to buy?"

"Could be."

Coop felt pressed. "I git the feelin' you ain't here 'bout no car."

"You are correct, *Coop*. I am not here about the car. Although, I hear you do a lot of buying and selling cars. Is that right?"

"Sure 'nough. Been good to me. Gits my bills paid. Love me some cars, too. Sumthin' wrong with that?"

"No, sir. Nothing wrong with that at all. But, I am interested in someone who paid you a visit recently."

Coop tensed up a bit. Naturally reacting, he took the flask from his overalls and took a pull. "Who did ya say ya was?"

"Oh. Forgive me. I didn't say. I'm Agent Bright-ling, Georgia Bureau," he introduced himself, extending a hand.

For fuck's sake, Coop thought. His mind went to the well, where it was cloudy, forgetting to shake the hand that was extended to him.

"Alright then, I'll just get to it. We have word that your wife went missing some time ago and you haven't seemed to be too concerned about it?"

Coop took a swig from his flask. "Yeah. Yeah, she

did. Wouldn't exactly say she went missin' though. Best I heard, she left and took up with some guy without sayin' a word. So, I took this up," he said, tipping the flask. "Happens all the time. That ain't why ya came all the way out here now, is it? To tell me my wife left me? Believe me, I know it."

Brightling studied him, knew he had used his leverage, and went for the real deal. "Well, that is a shame Coop. Do you happen to know the man's name or where he lives? Seems everyone knows everything around here. In fact, I was told *you* know everything around here."

Coop got angry. "Reckon I don't if my wife done up and left me without warnin'." He almost believed himself, the way he used that tone.

Brightling moved on. "How about Bates? Would he know anything about where your wife might have gone and with whom?"

"You mean Dixie? If he knows, then he knows. Ain't the kind of man goes 'round tellin' anyone his business. But ya already know that."

"Seems nobody goes by their real name out here, do they? Hard to keep you straight. Wasn't he over here a few days ago?"

Coop shifted his weight onto the truck, knowing a lie wouldn't help him. "He might have stopped by. I have had a lot of these lately," he said, shaking the flask. "I don't do much dealin' with ol' Dixie."

"Yes, I know that. Which is why I was wondering what business he had visiting you…"

Coop wiped sweat from his forehead and thought a bit. "He was lookin' to find out if I knew where Billy went, I 'member that."

Brightling paused for thought. "Billy? Oh, you mean Billy Pierce?"

"Yeah, Billy Pierce."

"Didn't he leave town recently also?"

Coop reasoned with himself that telling most of the truth was the way to go this time. "Mm-hmmm, he left town."

"Do you know why?"

"Nah, just know he left. Sold him a car the day he did."

Brightling looked around the yard and stretched his hand out to Coop for the second time. This time, Coop shook it. Brightling held Coop's hand firm. "Seems like a lot of people are leavin' town....and you don't have many cars left."

With that, he turned and walked back to the front of the house. Coop heard his car pull out of the drive. So Coop went to drinking full on.

CHAPTER FIFTEEN

The day was routine by Watts's standards. He drank his coffee, already sweating under his buttoned collar, a thing he had gotten used to since the Bureau was in town. *Buttonin' up a shirt don't make a good cop*, Watts would think to himself. They already thought of him and his "police force" as a bunch of dumb small-towners, incapable of upholding the law or even putting a proper sentence together. While the Big Georgia boys had their accents, the small Georgia boys damn near needed a translator, or so they were told. So, he would dress to the letter of the law and didn't take it too personal. He knew he had a handle on what was happening in his town. He just didn't know what he didn't know, and he couldn't be faulted for that, rightly.

The phone rang on his desk, startling him. The

phone hadn't rung much until they came to town. Mostly, before Sheriff Morton was forced to resign, Watts and company were out, cruising around, keeping people in line, best they could. Usually the *same* people, but still checking in on them none-the-less. The shooting and the fire were the biggest things to occur out in the open under his watch, and because they had happened so close together, he knew that particular series of events was the trigger that tripped the bureau into final action. Sort of like dominoes. People and places, lined up in a seemingly quiet and identifiable order, but where they were and why—purposeful. He saw each event happen, one falling into the next, and so it would go until everything was in disarray and you couldn't tell what was there to begin with.

While they had their own makeshift "mobile office" that would never be mistaken for anything other than a run-down trailer with darkened windows—an odd man's escape or a poor family's home, perhaps—their target board, or a replica at least, had made its way into the backroom of the small, local station. Watts's space, since he was acting interim. He wondered how many of those target boards existed based on the same network of events. Not just in his neck of the woods, but in the entire country. He had heard about Oklahoma. He had read about Texas, even. They may have been out in the sticks according to everyone else, but people talked. These people, in particular. The Bureau. It was their job, and it wasn't. He knew they told him only what he needed to know. He was small potatoes to them, but he could shoot some fruitful sprouts, and they knew that also. This network was bigger than this target board, and if he were to be completely honest, he really didn't want it in his station. But it wasn't up to him anymore, what was going on in Winder, Georgia, except for traffic violations and your run-of-the-mill, every day "drunk and disorderlies", a sidewalk pisser here and there, of course.

But those weren't the things that gave Watts nightmares. Courtrooms, testimony, oaths and revenge. Those were the bane of his sleep processes. He had known James Bates, Billy Pierce, and Coop for a long time, and while he could never prove he knew anything specifically evil about Bates, he knew enough to know he had power over the others, the untouchables. And that was enough to know he should know more, enough to be called to testify, should they nab Bates. He was an officer of the law, after all. It was his duty. He would fulfill it, if called. But he wasn't sure he would fulfill anything else afterwards. He never fully believed Officer Short left town for good that night the abandoned barn burned down. It didn't quite add up. And Bates was in the back of his mind the whole time. All the same players, and no answers all the same.

Lost in thought, the phone on the desk might have made the tenth ring when he cleared his throat and answered. "Watts."

"Watts, its Agent Brightling," he started, same as always, as if "Agent" was his first name.

"Yeah, what say?"

"Goddamn, Watts. You sound like you just came from the farm. Speak English, man. Anyway, it's time. Today is the day… we are taking him in. It's a done deal."

Watts paused. He knew "him" was Dixie, or to the Bureau, James "Dixie" Bates, but he hadn't known of any event that may have transpired to make Dixie ready for the slam. "Today? What ya got?"

Brightling laughed. "Watts, you just worry about your shit, and we will take care of this. I'll be in to brief you before you lose your mind. But I need you not to do that, you hear me?"

"I hear you. I imagine some folks will be riled up at all this, what with it being a surprise and all. Reckon' you might get in here to tell me what's what sooner than later?"

"I'll be there," Brightling closed perfunctorily and cut the line.

Watts held the phone in his hand, looking at it as if it was the first telephone receiver he had ever held, and his heart rate sped up. *Today is the day*, he repeated in his mind. *Ahh hell.*

CHAPTER SIXTEEN

Dixie was at the old ESSO turned EXXON station—the same one where Billy had earned his first working dollar—buying a carton of smokes and some cold ones in celebration of Coop's sheepish divulgence of information. All he really needed was confirmation that Billy had left and wasn't hiding out somewhere trying to skirt Dixie's demands. Instead, he had enough information to make sure he wouldn't be challenged again. Ever. He was downright tickled as he walked out of the store that day. As he heard the jingling of the bell attached to the door ring behind him, he was so lost in thought that he didn't see them. Not one of them. In fact, it wasn't until he was already lighting up a smoke and cracking a cold one that he stopped in his tracks.

How many of them were *actually* there, he could

never say. Looked like a hundred, in hindsight. Surrounding the lot and the store, all cars, persons, and guns trained square in his direction.

"Hands up, James Bates. GBI!"

Dixie put his bag on the ground, slowly raised his hands shoulder height, cigarette still clinging to his lips, and smiled. "Well, hey y'all. What's doin'?" without hesitation.

"Cigarette break's over. Now spit that cigarette out, boy!" someone yelled, guns still trained on him.

"Sure thang...gonna have to use my hands though," he taunted defiantly.

"Spit it out. NOW! This is not a joke, James."

He felt it. It wasn't a joke, and it wasn't local. What the fuck was going on? He spit his cigarette out, hands still up by his shoulders. "I don't want no trouble. What the fuck ya guys want?" He scanned the crowd, seeking a familiar face to feed his fury.

As soon as his cigarette dropped to the ground, two large men he didn't recognize were on him, and they were rough. Slamming him to the pavement with his hands behind his back, one of them said evenly, "James Bates, you are under arrest for the murder of Terry Gentry, Abigail Gentry, Amelia Gentry, and Simon Gentry."

"Who the fuck you talkin' 'bout?" Dixie hissed. He knew, of course. He knew immediately. But he wasn't going to say a damn word to any cop about it. Not without looking them in the eye.

They read him his rights while he bucked a bit, not listening to a word they were saying, and as they were about to stand him up, the officer on his left side shoved his face onto the ground, onto the lit cigarette, and whispered with closed teeth, spit hitting Dixie's good side, "Don't think we don't know about Short either."

Dixie wouldn't give them the satisfaction of wailing in pain the way the cigarette burrowed into his skin from the concrete, but the wound was evident when they finally got him to his feet. They all felt he deserved more pain and less pity than the standard law breaker.

"Ya'll got the wrong guy," was all he would say. But he was thinking already. What was that lawyer's name? The one who would do whatever for whatever? "I'll be lawyerin' up. You best believe. Don't be askin' me no questions."

Brightling walked through his crowd until he was face to face with the man he had tailed and trailed. "Good luck that will do you. You are going to fry, Bates. Seems one of your little 'associates' got caught with Gentry's wallet, and what's worse? He is singing like a songbird," he said with a smile. "Do you know about songbirds, Bates?"

"Name's 'Dixie'," he muttered, growing visibly angry.

"You see, Bates, some songbirds, they don't have much to sing about, but they sing anyway…soft kind of. But others, they have so much to sing about, they are loud and large, and they just don't know when to shut up."

Dixie huffed. "What the fuck you tellin' me 'bout birds for?" he said, still playing dumb.

Brightling shoved him into the car and leaned down to look him in the eyes. "Oh I was giving you some history on the songbird, but mostly, I was just fooling. These aren't birds at all, and they sure aren't songs. You are fucked. You are done."

Watts walked slowly to the back of the cruiser and

leaned towards the open space that had been cracked for air in the swelter. He met Dixie eye to eye and smiled, just a little. "Got ya ol' boy. Got ya before ya got me, ya sick fuck." Dixie looked a bit surprised at the statement. "Yeah, they told me all about it," he said, referring to the rumor that Dixie had placed a bounty on his head but wouldn't do it himself.

Dixie locked eyes with him, and his mouth wrenched into a wicked smile. "Day ain't over yet."

Watts slammed his palm against the glass in front of the most un-human look any man had ever given him in all his years on the force. He knew they had the right guy at the right time. Finally, they had him. And maybe, just maybe, the town could rest a bit easier.

CHAPTER SEVENTEEN

At first, he didn't know for sure who tipped off the pigs *or* the hogs that day, but he certainly had a list of people he may or may not blame for it. It didn't really matter in his mind who it was, but it did matter that it happened. And it mattered more that it un-happen. He would get loose, he vowed to himself, and when that day came, hell would come calling, in person, on some folks.

The guards knew not to shove him in through the opening in the bars. They had been told Dixie was coming and how he was to be treated. Somewhere, someone owed him a favor. A lot of someones if he was taking a head count. Even in shackles, which wouldn't be on him long, he was already feared by all the others and most of the staff. *Favors.* After what he had done, nobody was about to treat Dixie like a regular member of the population, although they already weren't following protocol. They did, however, want him to sit, wait, and wonder. *Who? How? When?* So he did, in the place that time stood still but flew by at the same time.

When they finally granted him the luxury, the interrogation was anything but routine. Dixie didn't lawyer up for it the way he had threatened. He didn't cry or plead or deny. He didn't even appear to be uneasy in any measurable way. Dixie just listened to what they had to say, or mostly what Sam Roberts had to say, about the day the Gentry farm burnt to the ground. A recorded version. He listened to all of it. Occasionally, he would ask them to pause the cassette tape on the old black recorder and play it back. He would move easily between faces of rage and delight as he listened to his former follower, cohort and creation divulge everything that had happened from the night at the bar when they discussed and decided to rob the Gentry farm to the day they actually made well on their demonic intentions. His reactions weren't born from fear or shock or hatred for what was happening, but rather, they were his natural reactions of reliving the events, the way he had felt when they happened. It was a sight to behold.

They had gone way further than what was planned that day, of course, but none of that made a difference to Dixie. It tickled him, a little, to hear the version Sam told. It lacked luster. It lacked the feeling of the day's events, and it lacked anything resembling Dixie's trademarks. *That boy couldn't tell a story if his life depended on it*, he thought as the tape played itself out.

"So you see, Bates, they are on their way in with Jensen too. You are cooked," Brightling said.

Dixie knew it to be true. Freddy Jensen, the last of the trio that had stormed the Gentry house that day. Not known to be the smartest of men, Freddy would do anything for Dixie, but only out of fear. And that same fear would make him a little pansy-ass when he heard what Sam had already told them. So, Dixie knew, not that he was "cooked" as they had put it, but that they had hooked him this time. *Loose lips sink ships*. And lips around him had become way too loose. And while word got out, the fear and knowledge of the law's involvement would create more of those "songbirds" the agent was droning on about. So, he took it like a man. A sick and twisted man. The kind of man he truly was.

"You might want to be pushin' that button." Dixie nodded to the tape recorder and waited.

Brightling put a new tape in the recorder and hit the button. "Yup. I was there. Longer than ya know," Dixie started.

"What do you mean by that?"

"Well, ya see…we was there for the money they got for them cattle, just like Dale said. But that didn't go too easy. Ol' man Gentry didn't want to give it to me. He knew he didn't have a choice, but he still stood his ground…best he could anyway," he chuckled.

One more agent entered the room, leaned against the wall, and crossed his arms. Protocol. Just in case Dixie went rogue, he knew. It didn't faze Dixie in the least. He kept on. "His ol' lady wouldn't stop cryin' and raisin' a fit, so I had to shut her up," he all but boasted. "She whined a whole lot less when she couldn't even talk," he said, making the motion of being choked.

They hadn't seen anything like him before. Neither of the men needed to ask follow-ups or lead-ons. They just let him speak. And speak, he did. As if he was presenting himself an award.

"He finally told us where the money was when he

couldn't stand to watch his wife buck and kick no lon-ger...." he paused. "Hey, say, think I could bum a smoke?"

Agent number two approached him, pulled a fresh pack from inside his jacket, and held it out to Dixie. "Sure thing. I'll even light it for you."

"Well, ain't that sumthin'. Whoever said the law ain't got no manners?" Dixie took his time puffing on his cigarette before he spoke again. "Where the fuck was I? Oh yeah, so he goes to get the jar where they put the cash and brings it back to me, but ya see, I kinda felt like he took too long and it was more a hassle than I wanted it to be in the beginnin', so I went ahead and finished his ol' lady off. In front of him. Her hissin' and spittin' was gettin' on my nerves."

The rage he had felt in the moment he took her life was evident as he re-told the story. But they let it go. And he couldn't help himself. He was proud. And if he was going down, he wanted everyone to know it. "That ol' man 'bout lost his shit when he saw her go. Hooooo-ey, did he ever! I mean, he tried to come at me, but the boys took him down. Wish they would'a let him. But he was on the ground when I said fuck it all and did him too. Same way. He didn't fight it. I'll give him that. Took it like a man."

Nobody said a word. They simply did not have to. They only had to listen. Simple as that.

He squashed his cigarette out with his pointer fin-ger, letting the skin burn, the smell rising from the ashtray, and leaned back in his chair. "We was countin' the money when ol' man's daughter and husband showed up. Now that was a surprise. We was plannin' on lightin' her up and leavin', but damned if that just wasn't what was meant to be," he almost delighted. He sat in thought, a smile on his wicked face, thinking back on the event he was recount-ing, revealing if he hadn't already, his true nature. "Y'all ain't very talkative," he looked at Brightling and then to the other, back at his station against the wall.

"If we have a question, we will ask," Brightling responded, straight faced.

"And Sam took her, and I took him. I snapped his neck clean, he didn't feel nothin'.'"

"And her?"

"Shit. Sam didn't have the balls to do nuthin'. He smashed a pot over her purdy little head, but that was 'bout it. Don't know if she came to or not, but we gassed that place, lit her up, and left…best two-thousand bucks I ever done made."

"Two-thousand bucks? In a jar? You did all that for a lousy two-thousand bucks?"

"Well, hell, I didn't know what they had, just knew they had made some sellin' them cattle. The rest…well, that was just…a lil bit o' fun. Necessity. Yeah, I know right words too, don't be thinkin' I'm dumb."

Brightling leaned forward. "James Bates, right now, I think you are one of the dumbest son of a bitches I have ever met."

"I'll be makin' a phone call now. Gotta call my lawyer." It was very untimely and unsettling, even to Brightling.

CHAPTER EIGHTEEN

Time ceased to move. It could have been an hour, a day, a year. It didn't matter to Dixie, and he stopped keeping legal time. For a while, it seemed trial wasn't even necessary, given the evidence and full confession, but it was a big one for those parts, none-the-less. A stage Dixie wouldn't relinquish if given the chance, no matter the ultimate consequences on the table. While he later recanted everything he had openly told them about what had transpired on the day the Gentrys met their fate and claimed to have been drunk and "just messin' with them", both of his cohorts had turned and were granted immunity for their full cooperation. In the end, the jury would be horrified, disgusted, and vengeful, just the same. The general feeling was that he had been caught this time, but he was certain to have committed many other criminal acts, none of which could be proven. He may have even insinuated as such, smiling back in the room with Brightling, but it wasn't admissible, of course. Because he was just that good at keeping secrets. Until now. Dixie wouldn't give anyone the pleasure of taking the stand in his own defense. He didn't care to be questioned again, and his lawyer had advised against it. "Trust me. It's for the best. All in the works, James."

Handing down the verdict on the murders was just as easy as delivering the sentence. It would be death by electrocution for ol' Dixie. Some would have preferred an old school hanging in this instance, they would say. But since it had been outlawed and thanks to a case they called Gregg v. Georgia, electrocution had been re-instated, along with the death penalty itself, just in time. And if anyone ever deserved to fry like bacon, it was this man, everyone figured. They granted the lesser—burglary and armed robbery—to make their point, each carrying their own weight in years behind bars. Most of them thought it didn't matter on account of his death sentence. Most of them would turn out to be wrong.

Dixie held a flat affect when he heard the decision from his so-called "peers". As he left the court room, he spat in front of them. Each of them flinched, as though his spit was venom and were it to touch them, they would surely suffer the same ill-fated, painful demise he was facing. But he had time. He had plenty of time before they flipped that switch, and he knew it. And he planned to make the most of it. People had to pay, of course…Roberts, Jensen, anyone he could name on that so-called "unbiased" jury, and anyone who would attempt to take his place now that he was on lockdown. He started keeping time again.

There was only one who came to mind who might think himself man enough to even attempt that, and Dixie knew he was just head-strong enough to disobey, now that he would surely find out that he was "safe". But he wasn't safe. None of them were. And they never would be. Dixie was madder than hell, and God help anyone who crossed him off because he was sitting in prison. He didn't plan to stay there too long, and as fate would have it, he would be one key closer to the front door within the first year. Connections and debt. He always had the first, and he collected the second for tough times. The right people owed up to their eyeballs. And it was time to cash in.

The first chip had already been paid, in advance, to the designated people, through his lawyer. He may have been sentenced to death, but by all the proper accounts and records, there was no room on death row. Dixie would be a permanent member of the general population.

CHAPTER NINETEEN

The walls were whitewashed—grey, really—chipped and stained from visitors and memories past. In general, it was a cold, hard, and empty tomb, permeating with not-so-subtle hints of chlorine and body odor. To anyone else, an assault to the senses. He never troubled himself with such things, however. Dixie knew the cage would test him, of that he was positive, but he also knew that it could not contain him. There wasn't a thing in this world that could contain him.

In an odd sort of way, he liked it, the sense of challenge it presented. Could Dixie rule and reign from inside those four flat and confining walls with seemingly limited resources? Of course he could. And limited resources were in the eye of the beholder. Dixie knew there was nothing, absolutely nothing, that he could not get his hands on with the bend of one single ear.

I just have to find the right one, he toiled. Following lightly with, *let the games begin*.

It took him some time, some serious role-playing, and sheer determination, but he eventually knew who was who and what was what. And of course, he was waiting, as he always did, for the opportune moment. Lying in wait, like the predator he actually was.

He determined there to be more than a million scams, runs, and plays on the inside, more than he was generally used to, which was a shitload best he could figure. But he could run with the best of them. In his mind, he *was* the best of them. And he may just have been. For some, he played innocent, for most he played...himself. The die-hard rules he already knew. He invented them well before he was in that shithole—stay alert and learn some manners, be assertive not aggressive, unless aggressive was required. And on occasion, it certainly was, but you had better be prepared to back it up, lest you lose life or limb. There wasn't a soul in that place that hadn't heard of him in some form or fashion, but most of them had only heard stories and whatever part he played in them, they believed. It was easier to believe he was the normal, run-of-the-mill, new guy, and the stories were all just exaggerations of some version of the truth.

He played them well. He was in his element when his fingers danced with their puppet strings. The more he knew, the better he slept. Like a baby, almost, when it came right down to it. And truth be told, he felt more grandiose inside those walls, around those men, doing what he did best, than he ever had before. They were becoming his. His everything. Toys, players, pawns, minions. Call it what you will, but they belonged to him, and that was how he needed it. He had things to take care of, and he was finding the right people to get those things done. It was only a matter of time before he would make some moves, he would think as he drifted to sleep. There were people on the outside he needed to visit, metaphorically speaking. And he wasn't about to let those people forget about him or his capabilities. He knew exactly who was delighted in his current state. Maybe not delighted, but breathing a sigh of relief, and he didn't do favors like that. No matter where he was or how many bars or locks were between them. *No sir*, he thought. *Can't escape ol' Dixie*. The thought brought a hellish grin to his lips that always lulled him to sleep. If sin ever really sleeps, that is.

He would have to choose an example. Someone to take a hard prison fall to prove he was who they had heard or even thought he was. And he had just the man for the taking. Dan, two cells down. He was older, tended to rant about demons and conspiracies. He cried a lot, had a tendency to be a loner, mostly because people couldn't handle him in large doses but a little because he wasn't one to trust others easily, especially in this place. Dixie had used his friend face to get on with Dan, to gain his trust, and listened to well over his limit of woes and sad tales of solitude. He was downright ready to put him out of his misery when it came down to it. Nobody would miss him, and everybody would believe the appearance of what Dan had done to himself.

Except Dixie would make sure word would spread amongst the general population about what *may* have really happened, and once it did, nobody would say a goddamn word to anybody who mattered, or they were sure to suffer the same fate. It was a simple statement of hierarchy and ability, really, and Dixie was never anywhere but at the top of those mountains, on the inside or elsewhere.

****

On a weekend when he was feeling particularly ant-

97

sy and more like a caged animal than a man, Dixie decided it was time to make a move. People were in and out with their visitors, music was piping through to the pods, and nothing out of the ordinary had happened in quite a prison minute. He waged his time well with Dan that day, listening intently to Dan's mental woes and ailments, gaining his trust to the point Dixie promised him he would help him outside the limits of the rules, and Dan perked, a little.

"I'll see ya tonight, Dan. Don't know how I'll do it, but I'll git to ya, and I'll have sumthin' that will make ya feel better. I promise."

Dan looked despondent. "They already give me that junk to make me feel better, and it doesn't do anything for me…thanks though."

Dixie grabbed his hand, held it tight like a best friend would do, and looked right into his saddened eyes. "This ain't the same, Dan. I can make you better. Trust me?"

Dan hadn't had a real friend in what seemed like forever. The way Dixie held his hand felt reassuring. "I trust you. Thank you, friend."

"Ain't no problem 'tall, Danny boy. You rest now. I'll see ya t'night. Don't ya go tellin' nobody. I don't wanna git in trouble for tryin' to help sumbody."

"I sure won't. I sure won't."

Dixie left the common table and grinned all the way back to his own cell. *Check one*, he thought.

When the guard came down the row, as scheduled, Dixie mentioned casually that he enjoyed the music and wished he could hear some of the vinyl records they had been playing that evening at lights. "Helps me sleep… 'specially them Rollin' Stones," he said. The guard said he would see what he could do. They enjoyed him, of course. Dixie was their best friend when he wanted to be, the model of the pod, a cut-up, a reformed criminal who had obviously gotten a bad rap. After all, *who gets off the row so quick and easy*? Or ever, for that matter?

Check two. He delighted. One last step—the big one. Dan's celly. He wasn't easy to talk to, not even for the slickest slug in the patch, but Dixie already had him filled with dreams and promises. He had already agreed that if Dan needed Dixie, he would trade places before the bars locked down and the lights went out.

With ten minutes to lock and lights, Dixie snagged him. "Hey, Johnny boy. Guess ya seen Dan's all worked up today."

"Yeah, I know. I really can't take any more of his crying and whining. He is driving me nuts. Being here isn't bad enough? I gotta be with the biggest cry-baby on the block? Fuck me."

Dixie made his move. "I'll switch ya for the night. He listens to me. Stay in my cell, lay down, and face the wall. Ya know they never check. They only count. And in the mornin', same shit. We walk out, they never knew we switched. You will sleep like a baby, and I can handle Dan. Consider it a favor."

"Fine by me. Isn't like I'm going anywhere any-way. And I sure would like a night without the blubber-ing."

Then stay here because we 'bout ten minutes from last call.

"I'll be asleep before that even happens," John said.

Dixie patted him on the back as he shifted two cells over. *Check Three*.

And it went exactly as expected. Everyone was accounted for in their cells, numbers not faces. Cells were locked down, and lights went out.

Dixie whispered kind words to Dan, who felt comforted by his presence.

"How 'bout that music?" Dixie yelled when the guards returned to their stations. And the guard he had kindly asked, like an older gentleman, to play his favorite record, put his favorite song on. And even cranked it up a bit.

While Dixie wrapped the celly's sheet around his own hands in the dark and covered his torso with the other like a gown, he listened to the Rolling Stones sing about "Dancing with Mr. D" and to Dan one last time, mostly to agitate himself. As the fitting tunes played, he covered Dan's mouth with the sheets and secured his upper torso with his pulsating strong arm, and the fork Dixie had taken from the commissary went to work on Dan's wrists. Even if they could hear Dan over the kick and pitch of the Stones, they would think nothing of it. He cried and sometimes even wailed all night, every night. But on this night, the crying stopped. And when it did, everyone slept peacefully for a change. And in the morning, he slipped out and was counted in place, same as John. *Check mate.*

"All it takes is one bad day to reduce the sanest man alive to lunacy. That's how far the world is from where I am. Just. One. Bad. Day."

~Alan Moore

CHAPTER TWENTY

Kathleen met Jocelyn at a meeting she heard about through her church. "Parents Without Partners" is what they called it. While it sounded awful to Kathleen and only half true, she couldn't help but feel the urge to find someone, anyone, she could relate to, or vent to, or simply be around who might understand an ounce of her current situation. Billy would have hated the idea and forbidden her from going. It made him sound like an absentee father. And in his mind, he wasn't absent if he was sending money, which he was. But Kathleen had grown tired, lonely, and heavy-hearted once again. Knowing that Dixie had been locked away, the way it had all been put on public display, she couldn't fully understand why Billy hadn't returned, save to create a version in her mind where she was still in some type of danger if he did. It wasn't entirely implausible.

Maybe he didn't know, she would reassure herself. But she knew better. If there was information to be had, Billy had it, and if he didn't, it was only because he didn't want it.

Dixie was and always had been more than one man. And the thought of him still made her shudder. Kathleen would reach out as best she could. And a hand came back to her. Her name was Jocelyn Somers. She was a single mother of two. A real single mother. Her husband had split the minute baby number two came along, and she had been on her own ever since. And she was doing it. Better than Kathleen felt she was doing it, and she, herself, was still married—at least in her heart and on paper. Got checks in the mail, to boot.

"Ya still alone with three kids, Kathleen. It ain't no different, 'cept for the checks," Jocelyn would point out. "Y'ur doin' just as good a job as me, friend." She would nod over at Buddy, Jo, and April while they played with her kids in the small park created in the center of her apartment complex. "They're good kids, Kathleen."

Kathleen appreciated their similarities and, more so, Jocelyn's honest nature and open heart. She was a giving friend and always willing to listen to Kathleen about anything and everything that needed to be said for her own mental well-being. She even agreed that some people just love each other differently, or the best they know how.

"It ain't nobody's business but y'alls how it works for you," she would say and wink at Kathleen when she felt like she had to explain why she stayed with Billy.

Kathleen would have to get a voice recorder Jocelyn had told her. That way, if Billy did call and she was at work, he could leave her a message and she would know for sure. Jocelyn was always sure Billy had been calling, just always when Kathleen had been at work. "He wouldn't not check in on ya like that," was her reasoning.

"He loves you guys. He takes care of ya financially, still. That's better than most of 'em. Bet he misses ya sumthin' fierce."

That may have been true, but Kathleen wouldn't be getting a recorder. She didn't want to hear the silence over again that she heard from the telephone as it was. She preferred to believe that he was calling when she wasn't home. There was no need to confirm he wasn't.

Of course, Kathleen hadn't told Jocelyn everything there was to know about Billy, their marriages—plural—or any other bit of information she didn't really need to know, but for the most part, Jocelyn got the gist. He wasn't there, after all, and Kathleen had to tell her at least the basics, albeit a somewhat altered version. And it wasn't like Jocelyn didn't have ears. Being in the same general area, around the same general folks, because they were all there was, she had heard of Billy Pierce. *Who hadn't?*

Kathleen hadn't actually heard from Billy in quite some time, besides the cash that came through Brother. She knew what that meant. Billy was protecting her, yes. But she also knew he was keeping himself busy and *entertained* without her. It was in his blood. She shuddered to think about all the things she didn't or couldn't know. It was better not knowing, she had decided long ago, for herself and the kids. Raina had helped her come to that conclusion. There wasn't a doubt in her mind that he loved her nonetheless, and in the end, it was her he would always choose for keeps. So, if whatever or whoever was stealing his time kept him happy in the interim, she would just have to let it go, *wouldn't she?* She had more important things to keep in order besides her heartstrings. Her babies, the true and pure blood in her veins, the reasons she rose every morning and made it through every day without him. They were a piece of him, after all. She could see the best, and the worst, of Billy in each of her children in so many ways.

Every day he was gone was a day Jo became more Billy than Kathleen. Her look, her sass, and her defiant nature—all his. When Kathleen would successfully put her worry for Billy out of her mind, Jo would whip out a phrase, shrug her shoulders, and say with a venom only Billy could have produced, "That's what daddy woulda done," or "Daddy woulda said that".

The stingers. Jo was just as good at them as Billy ever was or could be. And they were meant to hurt. It was Jo's own way of expressing her anger or loneliness, so she couldn't really be faulted. She had learned from the best, after all.

April was quieter, more subdued. Mature beyond her years, she tended to things and didn't say too much at all. She was a gentle girl and had become quite detached since Billy had left. She was becoming her mama in so many ways it made Kathleen both proud and fearful. It was nothing for April to pack Buddy's lunch, as well as her own, walk him to his school on the way to hers, pick him back up on her way home, and have laundry and dinner going by the time Kathleen got home from work.

Jo would disappear with the older neighborhood kids most of the time, and when she did spend time with the family, she tended to disappear mentally all the same. Kathleen only knew what she knew because April would keep her informed.

Kathleen would vent to Jocelyn when she was worn out from Jo's antics and petty games.

"You need to keep that girl busy, or else she ain't gonna git no better," Jocelyn would tell her. "She might already be too far down in her own mind. Anger does that to ya...I've been thinking on an idea. What if we started a garden at your place full of fruits and vegetables? Spices even. The kids could tend to it. Mine too. Play in it, build their own sumthin', ya know? It would keep them busy, and they would learn to work and how good it feels to make sumthin', bring it to life. Buddy needs more. Playin' in the dirt and tendin' to the garden would be good for him, but what about a pet? Doesn't have to be a dog or a cat? Hey, maybe some chickens? That would definitely be fun for all of them, and it all really works for us too, Kathleen. I could go for some fresh foods, and ya need sumthin' to be when you are home. A purpose. Ain't nobody done no good in life without a sense of purpose. 'Sides raisin' children, the best purpose there is, ya gotta have sumthin' else in y'ur life. Y'ur workin' too much as it is, girl. I know it gits ya out of the house when it's empty and lonely, but it ain't lookin' good on ya."

Kathleen listened to every word. "I know, I been runnin' from the emptiness. Just tired of wishin' and hopin', ya know? I think the garden is a right fine idea. I can see it in my mind," she said with a smile. She grabbed Jocelyn's hand, "Thank you. For caring. And for…just being 'round with the kids and all."

Jocelyn smiled. "Of course, what are friends for, Kathleen?"

And Kathleen couldn't say she ever really knew the answer to that question, so she smiled and went to talking up the garden, walking the property, and deciding on how to start.

The kids loved the idea. They worked hard to get it started and had incredible fun running around, digging in the dirt, and playing garden games with Jocelyn's children. The garden was a living production, and it made them feel alive. The way the garden grew, the way they worked together to maintain it, brought them closer and eased their wondering minds. Even Jo had a laugh and dirty hands a time or two. It would be short-lived, given the seasons and all, but it was more than worth it to Kathleen, and she couldn't thank Jocelyn enough for planting the first seed.

No matter how much fun, or how happy it made any of them, always, each of them in their own way, wished Billy could see them, help them, laugh with them, grow with them, and be more present than only in their minds. And each of them dealt with those feelings in very different ways.

CHAPTER TWENTY-ONE

Throwing up houses in Florida confused Billy's sense of the passage of time on account of the weather. He wasn't that far from home, really, but the seasons felt distinctly different. It hadn't felt like he had spent much time away at all, and at the same time, he knew that not to be true. It had been a particularly rough day on the jobsite, and he had even lost a few men due to the pace at which Billy commanded things be done. Walk-offs, they would call them, and although it wasn't that unusual in his line of work, each time was just as frustrating as the last.

Billy had long since told Brother to reach out to Kathleen, to let her know he was alright, and when Brother decided the time was right, using all the local information he knew, he should bring Kathleen and the kids to see Billy.

Brother had looked in on her from time to time, given her the money Billy would send for her, and report back that she was, "Fine, took a job, kids are growin' sumthin' fierce…" All things Billy wanted and needed to know, but Brother had said he would call when he thought it was a good time to bring them to Florida to visit. Billy hadn't heard from him since. And he felt a brush of insignificance cross his heart.

He had tried to call Kathleen and the kids and got no answer, which he always found frustrating. She was working, he knew—had taken up a job with Freight-liner—and his children were in school, Brother had said. Billy knew his cars and most news relating to the subject. Freightliner had been hiring like crazy. Daimler-Benz AG, one of the world's premier automotive companies and builder of heavy-duty commercial vehicles, had purchased Freightliner from Consolidated Freightways, and very quickly, vehicle sales began to rise. He hated her work-ing, but he didn't like the idea of her sitting at home with nothing to do either. They had been *there* before. His own indiscretions he could live with, but not hers. He simply didn't care for those memories.

Yelling to his current right-hand crewman, Billy gave it up. "Paul, what say we knock off this one and call it a day…go have us a cold one?"

Paul instantly dropped his hammer without speak-ing and headed towards the trucks. He turned around, noticing his response had been so sudden he hadn't really responded at all. "What do you say we do? Move your ass then!" He was an easy-going, good time kind of guy, and he had stuck through the constant turn-overs.

Not generally one to cut out of work, Billy bared no guilt on this day. He cleaned up his tools, loaded his truck, and yelled "Slingers!" out his window to Paul who waited patiently in his own truck. Paul gave the forehead salute in acknowledgment of their destination, and they kicked up the dust like they were headed to collect a million bucks on a winning lottery ticket.

Billy saw her the minute he walked through the door. Having moments ago been concerned for Kathleen's outings, which only consisted of work, the irony was not lost on him. Sure, he had been there what seemed like a hundred times before, but he was certain she hadn't. She was carrying a cocktail tray and had the perfect smile for someone who should be doing so. He found her mesmerizing, the way she moved easy through the bar, spoke kindly, and laughed with everyone, clothes fitting her body just right. He was only moved by Paul shoving him forward from behind. "What the hell, Billy? Haven't you ever walked into a bar before?"

Snapping out of his trance, he headed to a high top, never taking his eyes off the young beauty whose presence he swore he could feel. He glanced around so as not to stare and realized he wasn't the only one whose attention she was holding. Hell, he wasn't even one of few. Every damn swinging dick in that place had their eye on her. And yet, she seemed oblivious. Maybe she was, or maybe she just didn't care. She caught them out of her periphery as she was talking sports with another group of early-offs and excused herself to come to their table.

"Well, hi guys. My name is Lacey, and I'm sorta new here, but I can tell you aren't, so let me know your poison, and I swear I won't forget!" Her eyes danced and sparkled like emeralds.

Billy couldn't speak for a minute, so Paul piped up. "My boy seems to be having some sort of problem, so I'll go ahead and order two Budweisers, sweetheart."

"Well, alright then…" she said, looking at Billy for a split second longer before turning to leave.

Paul kicked Billy. "What the fuck, man? Where you at? Ahhhhh, I get it. You staring at that sweet little thing, aren't you? Well, you better forget it, Billy boy. She doesn't want anything to do with the likes of you, and if she does, well hell, something must be wrong with her!" He snorted.

"Nah. I was just wondering where she came from. Seems like there's been the same people here since, well, since we started coming here. Haven't seen her 'round town neither."

She was back with two, cold long-necks before he could finish what he was saying, and again, she caught his eyes, and he was knee deep in hers. The way her hair fell across her face, he felt like he knew her. Not possible, of course, but he couldn't shake her from his vision, no matter how many times he shifted on his stool.

"Damn man, I have never seen that look you have on your face right now. Wasn't sure you had it in you, actually. Wife and kids and all..." Paul trailed off under Billy's glare.

Billy was colder than Paul had ever heard him. "You ought not mention my family, Paul. Ever."

"Alright, Billy, it's cool. Shit."

They were about a sixer in when Paul decided he was done. Billy wanted to leave just the same but felt glued to his chair. He had interacted with Lacey a few times for a few seconds at this point, but something was definitely there, and while he tried not to entertain it, her eyes wouldn't let him go.

"I'm gonna stay a bit longer." Billy nodded as Paul got up.

Paul looked at Lacey and back to Billy with a grin.

"Yeah, yeah…I bet you are. She has flung a craving on you, hasn't she?"

"It ain't like that."

Paul tilted his head a bit and gave a nod, grinning from ear to ear. "It's always like that, Billy boy!"

Watching him leave, Billy wondered if Paul was right. Paul didn't know him all that well, but he was pretty much what Paul thought he was. But this felt different. Maybe it felt new. He couldn't tell the difference this time. For once, he felt no wrong in his want for this girl he couldn't remove himself from. And hell, he knew he could have her. Seemed like it might take some work, this one, but if he wanted to, he was certain she could be his. And he wanted to. *At least once, anyway.*

While he went through that thought in his mind, Hatchett and the boys showed up. "Thought we might find you here, Billy boy! It's time to discuss some shit, turns out." Hatchett swung his bar stool to motion for a beer and instead, jumped up and went straight to her. Billy watched her eyes light up and sparkle as she hugged Hatchett as though they had known one another for years. He envied what he saw.

Hatchett came back to the table with a round of beers and a smile on his face. "You treat that little lady like she owns this place and take care of her," he said, flashing his money and throwing some on the table.

"Ya know her?" Billy asked.

"Know her? Hell Billy, that's Whiskey Bob's sister. And she is the sweetest and cleanest girl in three counties… fuck, any county there is. I would put my oath on it. She's not much for the Club. She's a good girl. I know what you are thinking. Good luck to you. Whiskey Bob will have your ass."

"Anyone else?"

Hatchett shook his head back and forth, smiling. "You are free to try, Billy boy. Like I said, good fucking luck."

Ahh hell, Billy thought. This was going to be a thing. Whiskey Bob was, at best, a half-wit with a roaring need to fight at any given moment. Billy could feel it coming. He would have to take Whiskey to the carpet if he was going to befriend Lacey, or more, and he would have to trust that Hatchett and the others knew him well enough to know Whiskey Bob wasn't worth it, or was fighting over his sister. Unless, of course, it was more serious than a date with a Free Rider.

****

It was on that very same night that Brother called him, said there was news they needed to discuss. But Billy had drank far too many, watching the green-eyed girl at the bar, and he didn't feel like discussing anything. He felt far from home. In one single day, he had gone from heartache to this is where I want to be, same as he always did.

"Billy, listen to me. It's goin' down here. Dixie…"

Billy cut him off. "Brother, not now. I can't do this now. I just…can't…" he trailed off as he dropped the receiver and stumbled to the couch to pass out.

"Billy? Billy?" Brother figured a bad connection or some sort of outage and hung up. He would try again, he thought. But he didn't think Billy should come home anyway. Not straight away, anyway. Not enough time had passed. What would that look like? To Dixie, to the locals, to the GBI? Was anyone watching anymore? And how long would ever be long enough? There were no solid answers to all the questions each of them would have on the subject, and they probably wouldn't agree were they to come up with any.

He didn't and couldn't know all the evidence that ultimately put Dixie away. He could only know what they all heard, which was Dixie 'fessed up about the Gentry place after Sam and Fred already turned him over, but he took it back, and somewhere along the line, his lawyer screwed up or something, and it helped Dixie out in the end. However, he feared what he didn't know, same as Billy and Kathleen. And the gaps in his knowledge on the subject seemed huge. So, he would keep his place as the watchful eye and wait until he thought things were settled or knew for a fact they were.

He had spoken to Kathleen a few times, but only briefly. He didn't really want to get involved much past letting Billy know his family was alright. And she was always so sullen. There were too many unknowns, and she always wanted answers he couldn't give her. He didn't blame her for wanting to know. He wanted to know just as bad as she did, for the most part.

CHAPTER TWENTY-TWO

Billy's job had become a steady, all-around home-builder's dream. He had his own hours, his own crew, and plenty of cash coming in. But it lacked excitement, and he had already been doing the same exact thing for so long. Just not in the same place. He needed more. He dialed Kathleen, intending on making it brief. Just a hello, nothing that would get back to anyone, but he missed her and the kids and wanted to hear their voices. The job, the sweat, the daily grind always brought them back. *Stability.*

She picked up after two rings, and he buckled a bit at the sound of her voice. "Hello?" He paused. She asked again, "Hello?"

"Kathleen, it's me," was all he choked out.

"Billy!" she screamed.

He could hear the kids come wailing towards the phone yelling, "Daddy!" He imagined them shoving each other out of the way, trying to pull the cord from their mama's hand.

"Kathleen, I can only talk for a second. I just wanted to hear your voice and say hi to the kids. Have you been getting' the money I been sendin' ya?"

"Yes, where are ya? Baby, it is so good to hear ya talkin' to me right now. Like a dream. I wasn't expectin' it." She started to cry.

"Don't cry, Kathleen. I'm fine. I'll keep sendin' ya what ya need. That's all ya need to know."

Kathleen hushed her tone. "Billy, ya know what has happened here?"

Billy thought she meant at the house. "What happened, Kathleen? Sumthin' bad?"

"No," she almost whispered, hand over the receiver to block her words. "Dixie, they got. He ain't 'round no more. He ain't been 'round a good while, but sumthin' went on in court, or after court. Don't quite know what."

"That's enough, Kathleen," Billy admonished. "I'll git the rest from Brother. I reckon whatever it is ya tellin' me, it ain't over. Not by a long shot, but I'll git the rest. Put my boy on the phone."

He heard a scuffle, and then Buddy went to racing his mouth. "Daddy, Daddy, I miss ya so much and I have so much to tell ya and when are ya comin' home cuz' I got stuff to show ya too…"

"Hush boy. I want ya to listen to me," Billy scolded, even though he was more than delighted at the sound of his youngest. "You bein' the man of the house? You takin' care of those girls and y'ur mama?"

"Yes, Daddy. I am. I really am…but just until ya git home soon, right?"

Billy realized that "soon" was such a relative length of time at that age. "That's right li'l man. I love ya. Let me talk at y'ur sisters for a quick minute."

April came over the line. "Hi, Daddy. I miss ya."

"I miss ya too, baby girl. Ya take care of y'ur brother and help your mama out, just like I told him, a'ight?"

"Mmm-kay, Daddy."

"Put Jo on the phone," Billy told her.

"Jo left when ya called, Daddy. Sorry. But here's Mama. I love ya, Daddy."

"I love ya, baby girl," he said, a bit heartbroken.

Kathleen was back on the line. "What did she mean Jo left?"

"Billy, things ain't the same all 'round. These kids, they miss ya sumthin' fierce. They need ya. I need ya. Jo, she is gettin' tough on me. I'm tired, Billy."

"Not much longer. I'll git it all sorted. Then I'll be home. I gotta go now. I love ya."

"I love ya, Billy. Don't be too much longer," she said as he hung up. "Not much longer…I'll be home." Same as he had said when he left, which now seemed like a lifetime ago. She simply didn't believe it anymore.

She stood there, phone in hand for a minute longer, wishing he was still on the other end or, better yet, standing right in front of her. She asked the kids to go wash up, and

121

when they did, she sat in the hall by the phone and cried.

****

Billy found it a sad kind of funny how a simple phone call could take so much out of him. There was a gaping hole in his chest that needed to be filled with *something*. The crew was taking the weekend at a lake house they used on the regular. It was in a cove off of St. John's River, fairly secluded, and it was generally a smooth, clean, getaway. This time, though, they invited their women. Billy asked Lacey if she cared to join them since they all seemed to spend their time together anyway. He knew she wouldn't hang around the Outlanders outside of work, except her brother on rare occasion. It wasn't something she wanted to be a part of. She didn't want to be considered a "sheep" or a "mama" to them, nor would her brother let her name be run through that way. Those names were reserved for girls who would and should do anything with any member of the Club or all of them at the same time. Desperate girls who wanted to work their way into becoming someone's "old lady." It wasn't Lacey's nature. And for that, the Club respected both Lacey and her brother's wishes on the matter.

She hadn't committed to the trip, knowing full well the boss-man expected her to work. It was a last-minute decision to call Billy and accept. "Billy Pierce," he answered, almost missing the call as he was scrambling to get out of the house.

The voice on the other end was unmistakable. "Hi Billy. It's Lacey. I…I think I want to go with you guys this weekend. I need to get away...from stuff. Will that be alright?"

He eased himself up. "Sure, Lacey. I think the other girls will love havin' ya 'round."

She felt nervous and excited and relieved all at the same time. "Oh good. Except one more thing. I need a ride, if everyone hasn't left already. Chuck took my car." Chuck was Lacey's on-again, off-again boyfriend of sorts, Billy had noticed.

"Well, I'm just headed out the door. I'll come git ya if y'ur ready."

"I can be ready in ten minutes," she said, hoping she wasn't an imposition but realizing she would not have been invited if that was the case. She gave Billy directions to her apartment and hung up the phone to throw a few things together. She was getting out. And she was happy.

It had not been particularly hot, but normally humid, like any Florida afternoon in mostly any season. Like most nights in the South, except for the dead of winter. The mosquitos were few, luckily, but the air was heavy. Just another weight on their shoulders. The water, cooled by the downing of the sun, brought ripples to their open toes and cooled them down, just a little.

They all sat on the dock, some in chairs, some on their denim-covered asses, fishing and drinking beer all afternoon into the dark, with the haze of the moon casting sparkles across the water. Two by two they had wandered from the dock to continue their adventures up at the house until it was just Billy and Lacey sitting and watching the bobbers. Her skin glowed in the pale light from above, and he watched her as she pressed her lips to her bottle.

He wondered if they were really fishing, or if they

were fishing for each other. Getting to know each other, wanting each other in ways they should not have been. Her boyfriend was back home, and he thought she was with the girls. His wife was back home and thought he was working. He didn't actually know what Kathleen thought he was doing, but he didn't tell her for her own safety. It helped him to think of it in such terms, and he did want her safe. Of course, he was working, most of the time, but there was always time to spare, no matter how busy one was, wasn't there? And there was this girl, who was more like a woman than any he had touched, tasted, or made love to, besides Kathleen. He meant to know her that way. He felt his blood rising every time she looked at him in the dark, on the dock, *fishing for something*.

He put his fishing gear down, chugged the last few swallows of his beer, and grabbed her beer from her, as well as her fishing pole.

"What's up?" she asked, easily. Being there, where neither of them was supposed to be-in the silence and the calm of the sticky night air next to the water, brought a calm into her core she had not felt in quite some time.

"Let's head up. Everyone is probably asleep, so we can take over the T.V."

She felt her stomach flip a little and smiled up at him as she stood, her hand still in his. "The T.V.? Okay."

He pulled her into him with fire in his eyes, knowing they were both wrong. She let him force her close. She was going to be his, he knew. He was never wrong with his instinct. Despite her boyfriend, despite his wife even. She looked up at him. Her eyes glistened in the slightest way, and he knew he had to put his lips on hers. He felt her melt into him. Her skin felt hot and damp from the humidity. He kissed her until he was almost holding her upright as she wilted. She tasted sweet, soft, and salty, all at the same time.

She pulled away and looked at him, almost as if in shock. "T.V.?"

"Okay," he said, hearing guilt in her voice. She was a good girl. And he was a bad guy. It made him want her more. He guided her from the dock up to the house, and she clung to his hand as if to say she was in it with him, whatever "it" was.

The house had cleared when they came into the kitchen from the deck. He was right. "I'll take another drink. Something on the rocks, please."

He smiled. "There's my girl." Mixing the drinks, he paused and turned to her. Her eyes were already on him. "Y'ur sumthin' special, you know that? It has been a lot of fun gettin' away from ev'rythang up here."

She looked down, brushed one side of her long, golden hair behind her ear, then put her hands in the pockets of her jean shorts. He couldn't help but look at her sun-kissed legs. He knew everyone else had seen them a hundred times at the bar while she worked, but they looked different to him, he was sure of it. "Yeah, me too," she trailed off.

"But what?" he said, handing her a Beam and Coke and sipping his own.

She tilted her head and shrugged her shoulders.

He put his glass down and touched her chin, raising it up. "They ain't here now. They don't know. We are here together for a reason. Ya know it, and I know it. Let's be us. It feels good, don't it?"

She couldn't lie to him. To the one at home, some-how, but not to him. "It does." She put her drink down. "Kiss me again," she demanded in the sweetest tone imaginable as she grabbed his belt line and pulled him towards her until she was backed up to the kitchen counter.

And he did, fully and completely. They were lost in the kiss. Both of them. He began to lift her onto the counter when she pulled back.

"What is it, baby?" he asked.

"T.V.," she said.

"Record player," he responded and left her briefly to put some of the old vinyl on the Technics turntable.

Again, he felt her guilt. Again, he knew it was only a matter of time. She wanted him.

They drank their drinks and lay down on the couch listening to the music, talking, and laughing. He lay behind her, and the comforting presence of him put her to sleep. She woke to the feel of him brushing her hair away from her skin and kissing her neck from her shoulder all the way up to just behind her ear. It was blissful. Half dream, half reality. *How could my whole body feel this way?* she wondered.

She let out a gasp, still feeling as though she was dreaming as his hand ran up the outside of her leg to her stomach as she turned to meet his lips.

"We should go to our room," he basically demanded, knowing it was over. Her resistance was gone. He felt it on her. Her skin was hot, her breath was shallow, and her heart was racing. He was new to her, and she to him. And different than the others. Somehow…different.

She rose from the couch silently, looked over her shoulder to him in submission, and then walked to the bedroom.

He met her in the darkness in front of the bed and took her body as forcefully as he would dare to, kissing her as deeply as he knew she wanted him to. She pulled his shirt over his head in between gasps, and he easily slid her top over her head as she raised her arms for him. He kissed every inch of her skin before she sat on the bed and lay back, never taking her eyes off his shadow in the dark room. He reached for the button and zipper of her jean shorts, and she let him slowly slide them down her soft legs. She sat up again and did the same with his jeans, only slower.

Heart pounding, she pulled him to her, and they slowly began exploring one another. It felt new. So right and so wrong, at the same time. He gently slid his hand between her legs, and she arched her back in newfound and building pleasure. Sliding his hands into her panties, he felt more sexually charged than he had in quite some time. There was something about this girl. The way she responded to him. The way her body shuddered at every touch, the way her biology told him she was his.

"Y'ur juicy like a peach," he whispered into her ear as he eased the silk down her thighs.

"I want you inside of me."

Neither one of them could take it any longer. He did not hesitate on her request. He was making love to her and her to him, and every second was a secret. There in the woods, on the oceanfront, in the dark room, the two of them were becoming one. It was sensual, sweaty, and sexy beyond their experience.

She began to gasp a bit louder, and he placed his hand over her mouth, something no one had ever done. She felt sexier and more intimate, more ready to let herself go, than she had ever felt in her life. Her responses stirred his fever for her. He hadn't known a sensitivity like hers since he and Kathleen had first made love, and something in him re-awakened that night.

With his hand over her mouth to keep their secret, she orgasmed like it was her first time at the peak, and he responded in kind. He fell to her, and they lay there, skin on skin, kissing and both wondering what and why it had been so different for each of them this time. It scared her, even as it excited him. It was the first time any man had made her orgasm from sex. Just sex. And he made her responses more intense than any man she had ever known. But she had known a lot of boys.

CHAPTER TWENTY-THREE

In the same time Billy was soothing his wounds in the same way he always did, Kathleen was falling to pieces. Her job was her rock, and her children were her heart. The rock kept her feet moving forward, if nothing else would. Hearing from Billy had wounded her more than it had healed her. He hadn't said anything that she didn't already know. And not knowing made the distance all the more palpable. The changing of seasons made the garden a haunted memory, overgrown and half dead like most of the other joyful and fruitful things from days gone by that she could remember. Jocelyn had met a nice man who adored her and took care of her kids. And before too long, his work would move them to North Carolina.

"I'm gonna miss ya, Kathleen. Promise me you'll

take care of y'urself. However ya need to."

Kathleen hugged her. "I got kids. I ain't got no choice."

Jocelyn pulled back, holding Kathleen's elbows gently. "There are some things you can control, Kathleen. Whatever makes ya happy. Don't care what it is, ya do that. Live y'ur life, honey."

"You go on now. Live your life. I'm so happy for ya. Come back to visit us," Kathleen said as the kids were saying their goodbyes to their friends as well.

It was a sad day in their house for each of them, to see their friends go, but Kathleen was quick to point out amidst the sunken faces that God had big plans for their friends. That is how life works. They had to go, and the kids should be happy for them. They were receiving a blessing.

****

At work, she kept to herself, mostly, although many a woman and man had tried to entertain her with conversation. Most would give up and move on, dubbing her an introvert. But in the late hours, when her sister would watch the kids so she could pick up a few extra shifts, Freightliner security guard, Dale Duncan, would bring her coffee, or check in on her—yet leave her be. He wasn't much for forced conversation, but he was clearly and enthusiastically for talking to Kathleen, when she would let him.

She didn't pay him much attention, but she was grateful for his oversight of the facility, and her, at nighttime. He never let her walk to her car alone, and he never overstepped his bounds. "Just doin' my job, ma'am," he would say when she thanked him.

She was yawning and having a good stretch one

afternoon when Dale popped in.

"Looks like ya need a coffee. C'mon, take a break. You've been bustin' your hump for weeks now. My treat."

She looked at her watch and agreed. It was almost lunch time anyway, and she was going to need some caffeine if she was going to finish out this work day, help with homework, feed everyone, and avoid butting heads with Jo before she got to slip into bed.

She grabbed her jacket and followed Dale out of her office. "Breakroom is that way." She pointed right as he took a left.

"Yes, it is, but coffee that doesn't taste like mud is this way."

She hesitated. "I should tell someone if I'm steppin' out…oh forget it, they shouldn't care, I s'pose." She had devoted hours upon hours of her spare time to the company, and her boss and his boss adored her. They had given her an office, and she felt appreciated and important. She didn't think they would truly mind if she went for coffee, or even left for the day for that matter. She was thinking about taking some time off sometime soon anyway. She was always so tired, and with the thought of her overwhelming sense of sluggishness, she yawned again.

"Ya gonna have to stop that now. It's makin' me tired!"

They reached the double doors, and she realized she hadn't grabbed her car keys. "I need to go back for my keys."

"No need. We can walk. It's really just 'round the corner. For heaven's sake, Kathleen, ya need to get out of this building more."

She laughed, a little embarrassed. But the fresh air

and the sunshine reinvigorated her, and the feeling left her quickly. She enjoyed the walk. And the company. Having adult time, adult conversation outside the confines of the building, was a rare treat. Besides Jocelyn, she didn't have anyone except her family, and she continued to keep her distance, not wanting to explain her situation or defend Billy's decisions or actions, mostly because she was complicit and her marital choices were none of their business.

Over coffee, she got to know a little bit about Dale. He was a single man, a father who didn't get to see his child as often as he had wanted or planned when he and his ex had split. She had never been his wife and felt no tie to him, he said. He had many interests, a bit of an ego, and he thought the world of Kathleen. As he talked, she noticed for the first time that he was a handsome man with an easy way about him. He was an enjoyable conversationalist, and he didn't seem to want too many things he didn't think he already had in life. He asked her about things other than her marriage, wanted to know what her life outside the office was like, and what she wanted it to be, really. She found just sitting with him soothed her ache and woke her up a bit. *Careful*, she thought.

"Kathleen, I think I gotta tell ya sumthin' right now," he said as he flipped the check to handle it without question.

Kathleen paused from sipping the warm cup she was holding as if it were gold in both hands. "Okay...I'm a little worried, the way ya said that, but shoot."

He put his money on the tab and placed both arms crossed on the table, leaning in. "I know Billy."

She nearly dropped her cup. It wasn't the words. It was the way he said them. "So?"

"I mean, I don't know him, know him. Not anymore anyhow, 'cept the things ya hear. But I met Billy a long time ago at the old ESSO station. Matter of fact, we been for beers together back then 'cause we had some of the same friends. Hell, everybody had the same friends then."

"Well, that ain't no story. It's news, I guess, but it ain't a story. Unless there is more to it…" she said hesitantly.

Dale leaned back from the table and began to fidget just a bit. "Not too much more, just wanted ya to know I go back with him, but we ain't friends now. I know he's been gone though. Again." He emphasized the last word, looking at her as he did.

She looked away. "Yeah, well, that ain't nobody's business but mine." *This is exactly why I don't talk to people*, she reminded herself. Except, it was a reassurance more than a reminder. She enjoyed talking to Dale, although it had just gotten a bit uncomfortable. But the discomfort was a feeling. A new feeling. A fresh feeling. She actually felt human again because of it.

"Kathleen, I asked ya to coffee because I thought ya might could use someone to talk to. And I like ya…and you were 'bout to fall asleep," he joked to ease the tension.

She stared at him. *Handsome*. "Thanks for noticing," she quietly responded. "All three," she smiled.

She didn't have to wonder what Billy would think. He would lose his mind seeing her having a cup of coffee with another man. Whether he had liked the guy back when they supposedly went for beers together or not, it wouldn't matter to him. She was spending alone time—his time—with someone other than him. It also didn't matter if he was doing the exact same thing or worse. His feelings were his feelings, and she knew where he would stand if he made an appearance to voice an opinion. But he wouldn't be making any such appearances. So, she discounted his opinion and carried on about her business.

****

One coffee break would eventually become daily coffee breaks that would turn into a happy hour invitation. Kathleen got along easy with Dale. He was interesting and funny, and he took her mind off things she no longer had any control of whatsoever. If she was being honest with herself, which she tended to do more often as the years had aged her into self-awareness, she never had any control of any of it, except she could have left for good. Any time. As usual, she thought she couldn't stay away from him, but that was a choice she kept making, not a finite rule of life. And this time, she really knew nothing about his life anymore. But he was choosing it, that much she was sure of. It didn't seem fair or right, but those weren't terms they used anymore. Things were what they were, and they weren't what they should be.

"Oh, two drinks, and I'm already an open book. I don't go out much," Kathleen said to Dale as she prattled on about the kids and work.

"Not exactly an open book, but definitely a talkative one." They both laughed.

She looked at her watch as she sipped her wine. Jamie had agreed to watch the kids, feed them, whatever Kathleen needed. She hadn't seen or heard from Kathleen since Billy left, when they had briefly discussed Kathleen and the kids coming to stay with her for a short time. None of the family had, which they found odd but not incredibly so given the circumstances as they knew them, which knowledge wasn't all that much. Jamie had thought it a wonderful idea for Kathleen to get out for a bit, other than to work. Of course, Kathleen hadn't told her she was with a man. Jamie didn't even know Kathleen knew any of the men around town. Not in any way more than a hello

134

upon passing by. Kathleen preferred the privacy. It was her friend, her life, and nobody really needed a say. She said enough to herself about it. And always, she could hear Billy's opinion on the subject in her head. But he wasn't one to talk now, was he?

Dale complimented her consistently, about almost everything. She didn't mind it, but she wasn't used to it. It made her feel uneasy yet brought her a small sense of satisfaction. She was still desirable. It was nice to know. And she welcomed it the more he did it. Although he was as sweet to her as many had been, there was something about him, some undertone, she couldn't quite put her finger on.

"Another one of these, and you'll be carryin' me out the door."

Dale took the opportunity. "I best git ya another one then!" He had lapped her in drinks twice over.

"Y'ur a funny guy, Dale Duncan."

"I'm not tryin' to be funny," he said with a straight face.

"Dale…c'mon now. Ya know I'm a married woman."

He put his hand on hers on the bar. "Are ya though?" He took money from his wallet, threw it on the bar, and got out of his chair. "Wake up, Kathleen. What you got ain't a marriage." He started towards the door, leaving her speechless and brokenhearted. And for just a split second, Daniel flashed through her mind.

She collected her thoughts and her things and rushed outside after him, catching him at his car. "I'm sorry. I didn't mean to hurt ya or nuthin'. It's just Billy…" She started but couldn't finish because Dale's lips were on hers, and his hands were in her hair, holding her to him.

She allowed it to continue, it felt so nice. Almost like a first kiss. A very first kiss. He had strong lips, and he knew how to use them.

"I want to take ya home with me, Kathleen."

She was gathering her thoughts once again, which were far too many to hold in one hamper. "Maybe one day. Not today." She needed to see her kids. She needed to ground herself.

****

Dale and Kathleen developed an affair that gave them both a sense of love, or something like it. He was a very sexual creature, and he treated her like the woman she had become. He taught and tested her in bed like no man had even dared. He would tell her she was more fun, sweet, and innocent than any other woman he had been with, and judging by his skills, she figured that had been quite a few. He would be more aggressive with her when they were drinking, but it didn't bother her. So long as she was the only one, and she was, she found peace in the intimacy, in any form it would take.

She eventually let the kids meet him and play at his house. Buddy never really seemed to warm to Dale, but he did like his playful, fluffy dog, Henry, and his house. Dale had an odd but neat little place in Ellijay, Georgia he had built himself. Its distance from Winder was half of its charm. Dale even enjoyed the drive time. Itswas full of interesting folk art and trinkets but provided safety and solitude. It was a little boy's haven if the little boy had an active imagination, which Buddy always did. April and Jo didn't spend too much time at Dale's. As the days went by, they had an increasingly growing need for more feminine types of stimulation, and the makeshift house on blocks wasn't exactly their cup of tea. April would either stay at the family house, doing whatever work she thought needed done, or she would pal around the houses of her classmates. Jo kept her endeavors to herself, mostly, because if she told April, April told Kathleen. *They are just too young to be this old*, Kathleen would lament.

Never introducing Dale as anything other than her "friend from work", they carried on as lovers, as if Billy wasn't her husband and never would be again. She realized, of course, that might actually be the case, so it wasn't that hard to convince her mind or her heart if either went to complaining or asking questions.

She placated her guilt, with the facts: Billy had left her and the kids. Again. Billy had chosen not to tell her where he was. Still. Billy had barely so much as called since he had been gone. Disappeared. Billy was leading a life she knew nothing about, and his kids were growing up without him, while she grew older without him. Truth. She was tired, and she was lonely, and she was damn tired of being lonely.

The rest she told to God, who knew her best of all.

CHAPTER TWENTY-FOUR

"I got news for ya," his lawyer said over the phone and through the plexiglass.

Dixie didn't care much for the man. He was a money whore. The entire state of Georgia knew it. But he was crooked as hell and a good lawyer to bat, so he was the best kind of whore Dixie could use at that moment. "Well, if it ain't nuthin' good, then I don't care much for hearin' it."

"Oh, it's better than good. It'll be official sooner than later. Probably make the news all over the place. Nobody can quite figure it out. I'm sure you have facts that could explain it, but I don't want to hear them. You just hang in there a minute longer."

Dixie knew that if his lawyer was coming in to see

him with news, it was going to be worth it. "What the fuck else am I s'posed to do? I'm in prison, ya asshole," he spat in response. But on the inside, he was hopeful. The debts and favors being called for must have hit home somewhere. And that is why he kept his whore of a lawyer, because he was a liar and a cheater and felt no shame doing Dixie's dirty work whilst calling it "lawyering". Then again, Dixie wasn't sure there *was* another version of lawyering.

"Let me explain it in the least of legal terms I have got. Your appeal, Dixie. It got kicked back to the state court. I don't need to say, but you did some business with the judge, best I can tell, or he knows you outside of court in some capacity. Anyway, he overturned your death sentence. And now it's just sitting there, buried, and nobody is touching it. Appears you may just be too much, James Bates. I won't ask what or why he owes you...or how many others there are that feel compelled to save your ass. I am more inclined to believe they are of the belief they are saving their own. All you need to know is you aren't going to die anytime soon. At least, not the way they wanted you to."

Dixie delighted in the news but was not surprised.

"They also seem to think you may not have had the best lawyer for your case...maybe I didn't do a good enough job for you," he said, winking.

"I knew I hired ya for a reason. Good enough to be bad enough on purpose. Ain't that some shit?"

The lawyer grinned in pride over his failure. "I do what I can, so I'm not sure what you mean."

"Well, you ain't done yet," Dixie said, agitated at his smug sense of final success. Where anyone else would have been overwhelmed with joy and delight at the lucky break or turn in justice, depending on how one would look at it, Dixie felt like something was instantly lost when the news had been delivered him. A sense of urgency, maybe. An adrenaline rush to drive and thrive on. Dixie was sure he would miss it—the feeling that he was near death, every breath.

CHAPTER TWENTY-FIVE

While Dixie was dealing successfully with forced fate and favors, Lacey and Billy carried on in their own world, not so many worlds away. They kept their lake cove secret from everyone for quite some time, best they could tell. Billy knew if Whiskey Bob found out, he would do his clumsy best to slander, defame, or impugn Billy to the Outlanders in any way he could possibly conjure with his dim-witted intellect. But it might be enough, and *that* was enough for Billy to contain himself around others. He would make it to the bar to see her as often as he could, but she would treat him with the same manners and clean flirtation in which she treated everyone. She was a kind, intelligent girl with a fun-loving personality that drew people towards her. All kinds of people. Mostly, they were just having fun, but when you are a flame, you not only light up a room, you tend to draw moths.

Billy wasn't the only one who noticed J.J., a Sling-ers regular. He was a white-bred, well-dressed, obnoxious type who didn't know when to shut up or how to act around anybody. A real *dick*, Billy thought, the way he treated the staff and ran around the bar jumping into people's con-versations as if they had asked for the displeasure of his company. He fancied Lacey, it was more than evident, and he had to be told on several occasions by several different people to back off. He never heard it though. He used line after line on her, and she gracefully dismissed him, God love her. Billy was actually shocked J.J. didn't get his ass kicked on the regular, the way he carried on, but people tended to keep their noses in their own business unless, of course, they deemed it necessary. Billy almost went to Whiskey Bob about the way J.J. carried on, but who was he to say anything about Lacey's life?

J.J., drunker than a skunk, always left with his tail between his legs either from Lacey's rebuffs or some guy's threats and bow-ups. He was harmless, best Billy could figure, the way he had no shame and cowered to the slightest of the men. He had stumbled over to Billy's table once spouting off about the waitress, and Billy just looked around at his guys, shook his head, and said, "Nah…" J.J. looked like a wounded puppy dog and scampered off to the next table.

****

Billy and what was left of his work crew were throwing them back like they always did, and Lacey was tending to them just the same. It was on a rare occasion he purposefully let the guys go home before him, to their families, their lives outside of work. Things Billy did not have then, for more reasons than one, but mostly, he wasn't choosing to have it anymore. He knew Dixie was locked up, and most of his lemmings along with him. But Billy

144

was Wild and free again, and as long as he took care of business for his family monetarily, the draw to stay here was greater, for now. He wanted something.

When the last customer shoved off, Lacey looked him over. "Billy Pierce, you still here? Planning on staying all night, were you?

"I'm just gonna finish my beer, sweetheart, then I'll git' goin'."

Whiskey Bob came barreling through the door, startling them both. "Well, well, what's going on here?"

"Nothing, Bob, I'm just closing up," Lacey said, scurrying towards him and into the middle of his pathway to where Billy was sitting.

"Whiskey," Billy nodded, tipping his drink. He could feel the adrenaline rising, and he knew this was about to come to a head. It had to eventually, so he figured it might as well be now. Besides, Whiskey was alone, which meant Hatchett had been right. It wasn't a problem for anybody else. Why would it be? Lacey and Billy were "civilians" who could conduct themselves any way they saw fit.

"I know what's going on, Lacey. You have been spending time with this guy? You know he is married, right? What do you think he wants from you?"

"Easy now, Whiskey," Billy said. "'Fore ya go and say sumthin' y'ur gonna regret."

Whiskey pushed past Lacey and shoved Billy's high top out of the way in one swift motion. "How's that exactly?"

Lacey tried to pull Whiskey back. "It isn't your business, Bob! Now go home…or wherever you go, but just go!"

"Lacey, let go of me. Billy and I have something we need to take care of."

"I'm not a kid anymore, Bob. What I do with my life and with who is none of your damn business. I don't care how tough you think you are...or what you think you know!"

Billy got up off his chair. "Lace, sweetheart, go on now and take a break outside. We'll be done in a minute." He had added the "sweetheart" to sweeten the blow.

Lacey huffed in anger at them both, mumbling about "egos" and "adults", and stormed around the bar past the walk-in and out the back door.

Whiskey flipped a buck knife open. "How do you feel now? I'm serious, Billy. You need to stay away from my sister. Mind your own life. She deserves better. And because you knew better, you are going to have to pay. In blood. Just a little for now," he jeered, jamming the knife forward.

Billy jerked his own body sideways, feeling the sting across his arm as he locked his grip around the Whiskey's knife wielding hand, twisting it until it began to crackle. Whiskey began to moan in pain "We done?" Billy said coolly.

"You done messing with my sister?" Bob gritted through his teeth.

"I ain't messin' with nobody," Billy responded, twisting Whiskey's arm a little bit more.

Whiskey wailed, "Alright, alright, let me go. We're done."

Billy released Whiskey's arm and stepped back. Whiskey shook it out as Billy reached for the sting on his upper arm. Pulling back a bloody hand, he realized he had been cut by the blade in Whiskey's first go.

"Nah," he said. "We ain't done." He threw an upper cut that belonged in the boxing ring. The blood spatter made it to the ceiling, and the bone shatter was audible.

Whiskey fell to the ground, writhing and ranting in pain. Lacey came busting through the back door and over to the two men. Billy looked at her. "I guess you can git a towel. And some ice. We'll be fine."

Until that moment, she had only noticed Bob's busted face. Now, she was surveying Billy's arm. "Oh my God. What the hell? Both of you! Take care of your own damn selves," she said, turning to finish her closing duties.

Billy helped Whiskey up. "Ya 'bout done, NOW?"

"Yeah, I'm done. Doesn't mean I changed my mind." Whiskey spoke angrily and headed for the door. Lacey threw him an old rag as he left and tossed a clean bar towel to Billy when Whiskey was gone.

Billy tied the rag tight around his arm, watching Lacey go about her business as if nothing had happened. His eagle had been sliced clean through the middle, a sign he ignored. Maybe it was time to cut it off—soaring on high, searching for more, his present lifestyle.

She walked to the front windows, pulled the blinds, and locked the front door. All tasks he had seen her do before when she was closing the bar up by herself. But something was different in her gait this time. She had her eyes on him.

"Ya lockin' me in?" he said, laughing a little.

"Seems like it might be a good idea, seeing as how you are busting up people's faces. People I love, no less."

"Lacey, it was comin' for some time. He was bound

to find out, and ya know how he is…."

"Shhhh…I know."

She flipped the lights, all except the neons which set a glow across the bar that sent a message. She didn't care to tend to the mess they had created in their childish display of machismo. That could wait until morning. She poured her favorite drink—Amaretto on the rocks, two cherries—and walked slowly to the pool table, leaning up against it. "I know you have been watching me, Billy. I can't say I don't like it. You want to do something about it?"

"Haven't I already?"

She smiled. "Not since the lake…"

He looked her over. Sitting on the edge of the pool table, legs smooth as silk in her mini skirt, soft hair flowing down over her face, hiding those green eyes that had drawn him in. She was simply irresistible. He set his beer back down and walked toward her, tossing everything he had been out the window. Again.

"Y'ur so beautiful," he said. "I really want to kiss ya."

Her heart nearly leapt from her chest, beating so forcefully she was sure it could be seen though her top. "I'm nervous," Lacey said. "I know I don't act like it, but I don't know anything about you. And last time, well, that seemed like something else, someplace else, and I was… someone else."

"I think ya do know me…it's still me. What ya see is what ya git. Don't be nervous, baby doll," he said, now within inches of her body.

He leaned down and kissed her collarbone in the

soft, sexy style that made her mind swirl. Then, he kissed her where her skin met the low-cut lace on her chest. His mouth skimmed up to the middle of her neck, and finally, he brought his lips to hers.

"Billy," she whispered into his mouth, feeling faint.

"Yes, baby?" He resisted kissing her because he wanted to draw out the waiting. All the waiting and wanting. It brought back lake memories.

"I'm scared."

He softly put his lips on hers for just a moment, and she could feel the heat of his breath. He tasted the cherries from her Amaretto on her tongue. Then, he drew back. "Did that scare you?"

She gasped, "No."

He kissed her again, this time softer and deeper, and again, he asked, "How 'bout that?"

"No," she whispered.

He took the back of her neck in his hand and kissed her for real. Lacey melted against the wood and the felt. She was his in that kiss, and he knew it.

It delighted him to have entranced her in that way. She seemed like the young girl he once knew in Kathleen, before all the hurt and the betrayal had changed them.

He backed away and he took to the jukebox, as he had watched her do a hundred times when people requested songs, and then there was music. Old, good music. She loved those old songs. *So sexy*. She took a swallow of her Amaretto, put the glass on the table, and stood up. "Kiss me again."

He was there in a flash, with more deep and lustful kisses. His hands now controlling her completely.

"Make love to me," she whispered, begging.

He released her lips, her head in his hands, and looked at her. "With pleasure, baby."

She opened her eyes and looked into his as he slowly began to run his hand up the inside of the smooth skin between her legs until he reached her panties.

A charge seared its way into her soul. Her heart pounded at least three times its normal pace, and she let out a gasp, closing her eyes again.

"Would you look at me?" he asked, desperate to look into her dazzling emerald eyes.

She hadn't realized she had closed her eyes this time at all. It was completely instinctual to her pleasure.

"Yes," she whispered.

His fingers traced the lace and silk of her panties on the outside as her breath deepened and she fought to hold his gaze.

She wanted so badly to close her eyes and feel nothing but his touch, but she did as he requesed.. His gaze kept steely and calm.

He slipped two fingers under the wet silk, and she grabbed his shoulders, feeling faint yet again. His eyes changed from a lull to driven voracity. She knew why. She was dripping with her want for him, and he loved the feel of it.

"I can tell how bad ya want me. I had no idea."

"Yes…Billy…you," she said between breaths.

"How 'bout now?" he asked, teasing her with his fingers, making her innate response all the more obvious. Her body wouldn't lie to him. She knew that.

"Yes. More…every…second," she spoke through his kiss. "I want the real thing."

He lifted her onto the pool table, making his way between her legs. He took each of her legs, one at a time, and placed her feet on the table as well. And then his mouth was on her. And in her.

She felt nothing but his warm tongue as he held her ankles tightly in place. She arched her back in exquisite delights of the flesh.

"Oh my God…"

He didn't stop. He kept her in place as he pleasured her with his mouth in extraordinary ways until she reached the point where she couldn't hold it in anymore. Lacey trembled under his touch and climaxed with an intensity previously unknown to her. She repeated his name over and over until she was out of breath.

And then he was inside of her, before she could regain her bearings.

"Yes, baby doll. Here I am."

At the feel of him inside her, Lacey instantly came again. Billy took as he had promised, and his lingering scent intoxicated her senses. She had needed it so bad.

As if he had read her mind, he whispered into her

ear, "You need me."

"Yes. I need you. I need you."

He rolled her over and held her hands above her head, thrusting into her harder and harder until the feel of her took him also.

As he gained his breath and his bearings, he slowly kissed the back of her neck and eased away from her. "I wasn't expectin' that."

She lay there, replaying everything that had just happened, over and over, smelling her own skin and touching the places he had been. "I know."

She had felt and tasted like sweet nectar to him, and he wasn't about to let that feeling go anytime soon or give it to anyone else. He couldn't wait to have her again, but his feelings were overwhelming him, so his departure was abrupt. Maybe a bit too abrupt for her liking, he would soon figure out. She was strong-willed, but sensitive…like him.

****

Before Lacey was his, he split his time between Slingers and Night Moves, depending on his needs and wants. But all he really wanted was her, so his nights eventually became hers. He enjoyed waiting for her at the bar, watching that body in a tiny skirt and fitted tank top, just like every other red-blooded man in the joint. He knew he saw her in a different way than they did. He could hear them, "Nice piece of ass", or "I'd like to get some of that". He would smile and sip his drink, knowing he was the one who she would come to when work was over. No matter where he was, she would find him, and they would have each other. Occasionally, it would piss him off, the way they talked about her, but he wouldn't waste his energy on them. They didn't stand a chance with her. She wanted what she wanted and none of them could give it to her.

He finished his drink and waved her over. "I need my check...*please*," he said with a wink. They were, after all, a customer and a server to everyone else. Still keeping the secret they had started that private weekend at the lake. He knew the others were watching. She knew they were watching her body. She liked it. He knew that, too. A woman who knows she is sexy can have a profound effect on the opposite sex, he knew. Especially a woman who wasn't obvious about it. Add booze and a wink or a smile, and Lacey was in good business.

"Let me just grab that for you," she said and spun to print him a receipt from the register. He watched her walk easily back to his table, giving another table full of guys the "just a sec" signal. She pulled a pen from her pocket and used her drink tray as a desk.

"You writin' a letter?" he joked.

"Maybe," she said, looking up at him with those green eyes.

She slid the paper across his high-top and walked away. Looking down, he had a zero balance and five words — "*I need to feel you*". He felt his gut tighten as much as his pants. *Man, this girl has a way.*

He watched her taking orders at the table next to his, flirting her way into the guys' dreams, and still, she glanced over at him. He nodded slightly. She smirked a little and went back to work. He left and went home to party with his roommates until she got off work. He knew she would come.

The secret was out. At least with his roommates, or rather men who stayed whenever they felt like it or didn't feel like staying someplace else. And they both knew that would be enough in this small town. But in those moments, neither of them cared.

She would fall asleep in his arms again, soothed by the safe feeling of his body protecting hers, and in the early morning, she would leave. He would grab her hand as she stepped off the porch in the dawning light and pull her back to him, kissing her goodbye as she characteristically melted into him. No words were ever spoken.

Neither of them knew someone was watching from three porches down. And taking angry, mental notes.

J.J. was doing his best to keep it together, to stay on his porch, tanked up, watching the nightly circus a few houses down. In fact, he liked to sit on his little porch, just a skip away from Billy's, and watch life go by, but usually, he didn't really have a choice. Mostly, he liked to watch Billy's life go by. It was an entertaining one, to say the least. Parties, girls, booze, drugs, bikers...what else could J.J. ask for? That one was easy. He had asked for an invite, more than once, and been turned down every time. All he wanted was to participate in the fun. That and Lacey, of course. He *wanted* Lacey. And he deserved her more than that married, ungrateful, southern hick down the street who came out of nowhere just as J.J. felt he was getting somewhere. He wasn't, of course, but he didn't know the difference. He had made her laugh, once, and that was all it took for him to sink his weight into the thoughts of hooking her.

The sun was just coming up that morning, and J.J. was drinking coffee on his porch, trying to sober up before heading off to work. He knew there had been an all-nighter at Billy's, but he had grown tired of watching and went inside to drink with his jealousy. And when he re-emerged, coffee in hand, she was on Billy's porch and he right behind her, shirtless. J.J. watched with intensity as Billy grabbed her hand from behind, spun her around, and drew her back to him for a very passionate goodbye kiss. It couldn't have been the first time, judging by the way they melted together. They were definite lovers. Thinking and feeling as though they were all alone in those early morning hours, like most lovers do. She pulled away slowly, and as she left the porch, he held onto her hand until he couldn't anymore because the space between them was too great. They both went about their business with smiles on their faces.

J.J. was enraged. That bitch had flirted with him and taken his tips but played innocent for years now. He had tried and tried to win her over, to take her on one date, but she said she didn't date customers. *Lying whore.* From the looks of it, she wrapped those legs around people she barely knew—married men, no less—while J.J. sat there single and obviously interested. He spent that day dreaming of ways to beat the shit out Billy, to get through the men Billy knew, but in the end, he knew that wasn't an option. He would have to stay out of the bar to save his skin because if he got drunk and stupid with Billy, there were plenty of good ol' boys to get drunk and stupid with him.

Damnit all to hell, he thought. The anger churned and burned inside him like a raging inferno of fury. Many a bottle shattered against the wall in J.J.'s house under the droning hum of Billy's parties a few doors down. And every morning thereafter, he would watch and wait, clocking every sleepover, every kiss goodbye, every single one of *her* body movements, until he made himself go mad. Lucky for him, another man in another town had his ear to the ground and had a little something to say about the subject. And while J.J. had been watching Lacey and Billy, the man had been watching Billy, through a broad channel, and his goal was the same, metaphorically speaking.

CHAPTER TWENTY-SIX

John had attempted to steer clear of Dixie since the Dan "incident". He was scared, and he didn't want anything to do with the monster who changed faces like the devil he was described in church as a boy. But Dixie was never far off. And when they would engage in conversation, John was sure to oblige him in pleasantries, or knowledge, if he had any. He had learned long ago that Dixie had a hard-on for details about some guy named Billy he used to know before he got locked up. It was happenstance that the name even made sense in his mind when he last talked to his wife, months before. But he hadn't said anything. He wanted to keep it as a resource, a payment, should he ever need it.

John was from Jacksonville, Florida but had gone

down in Georgia for burglary, a crime he always denied. Same as most of them. His sentence wasn't as harsh as some, so his wife and kids had stayed back, waiting. During a telephone call home, his wife had prattled on and on about the girl she worked with and her new boyfriend, how he was married and from close to where John was, and how he got along with the bikers in town, like he was some big shot. She worried about his wife and wondered if John knew anyone who might know her?

"That isn't any of your business, baby. Leave it alone," he had warned her, after hearing the man had connections with bikers. It could only be the Outlanders, he knew, and that was some shit he didn't want to stir up. He wanted life to be easy after this, and he intended on going back to Florida, his home. But she had mentioned his name. Once. Billy Pierce. And that rattled his cage as well. It had to be the same guy. How many Billys from Dixie's small town would be in Jacksonville carrying on like Dixie said he would be, wherever he was? And John knew Dixie had ordered him to leave town. It was all in a day's conversation. Back when Dixie wanted John to know who he was, when he had his real face on, before he started changing masks to get what he wanted, all the information he needed to connect the dots was laid out on the table like a fresh line.

On a day that Dixie trailed him around everywhere he went, just to make him uneasy, John struck up a conversation. Payment to be left alone. "Didn't you say you were looking to hear about a man you used to know…a Billy?" he said, feigning pseudo ignorance.

Dixie's eyes lit up like a child at Christmas, and flames shot through them. "Now why would you bring that up, John?"

"Well, see, my wife works at a bar with a gal in my hometown, and the way she talks about those folks, she really doesn't have anything else going on. And… well… hell, kind of sounds like the same guy. Don't know what he would be doing in Jacksonville though."

"Jacksonville? I knew his ass would head off in another direction. You know his name's Billy?"

"She said his name's Pierce. Hangs with the Outlanders, shacking up with a pretty little waitress from the bar. Says he carries on like he isn't married. She hears all the gossip, likes to dish it too."

Dixie seethed with excitement. The second of his golden tickets had just arrived via unexpected telegram. His face changed, and he lunged forward. His grip on John's state-issued shirt, now soaked through with sweat from the simple conversation he was having with the man who he knew had sliced and diced Dan to death, could not have been tighter.

In his signature alpha move, Dixie drew his coarse face into John's until his eyes were piercing through to the back of John's skull and beads of sweat, trickling from the tip of his nose, could be felt and tasted on Dixie's cracked lips.

"Now you gonna git yur li'l wife to git me what I want, and you gonna git it done by next week," he huffed into John's mouth. "I want one of them biker boys, don't care which one, sittin' in front of me. I know Billy, and I know him all too well. He may be gettin' along with those guys right good, but there is bound to be one of 'em that can't stand him. I'll take any of 'em though. We come from the same stock." John writhed a bit but stayed in the uncomfortable space of Dixie's words. "Tell me ya hearin' what I'm sayin' to ya," Dixie demanded as he looked back over one shoulder, then the other. "You gonna end up like ol' man Dan if ya ain't…now wasn't that a sad state?"

John understood, of course. Everyone within those

concrete walls understood what happened to ol' man Dan, especially John, his celly. And everyone understood the State's suicide explanation would stand, and nothing would be done of it. One less chicken, one strong hen to rule the roost. It was working that way, and nobody on the outside cared enough about ol' Dan what's-his-name to ask questions.

John had forced the bloody memories of the fork, the sheets, and the salad that had become of ol' man Dan's wrists far from his mind. Until that moment when Dan's name spat from Dixie's mouth into his. Then the horrid scene and the fear gushed over the dam of his mental blockade. He squeezed his eyes shut.

"What's the matter boy, ya scared? Look at me. LOOK AT ME!"

John opened his eyes again and would swear Dixie's gaze went red with rage. "I'm hearin' what y'ur sayin'. I'll git it done. She'll git one here," he promised, not knowing how to deliver.

A smirk slowly crawled across Dixie's face as he released John's shirt from his dead man's grip and eased back into a relaxed posture. "Ya will, Johnny boy. Ya will."

And he knew then that Wild would feel the heat of his hands on something he held close. No matter if he knew, and he was sure he would know, that Dixie was behind those bars. Nobody would take his post on the outside, and nobody would forget he was still in charge, no matter his circumstance. He would make sure of it.

John meant every word he had said, and he would act on them. He would do as he had promised under pressure, Dixie knew. Because, unlike him, John planned to get out of the slammer someday, and he would prefer to get out on his feet, not his knees. And if he delivered, he would be free from Dixie's constant surveillance, having pleased him with such a gift.

John's hands shook as he dialed the numbers on the raggedy old phone. A tear slid down his cheek as the line rang through to the other end.

"Hello?"

It was her. "Hi, Baby. It's me."

"John? Well, hell you haven't called in about a month! What's going on? Me and the kids have been worried sick. Almost drove all the way up there, but you know I can't leave work…and the kids have school."

"Yeah, Baby, I know, I know," John said, wiping the sweat from his forehead and switching hands to hold the phone with the hand that hadn't yet soaked itself with his sweat. "I can't talk long, Baby, but I need you to listen."

"You don't call, and now you want me to listen?"

"Baby, I don't have time to explain. Just trust me, okay? This is important. More important than anything. Do you understand?"

There was a pause. "Well, now I'm starting to get worried. Should I be worried?"

"Damnit, Baby, listen! I only have a few minutes, and I need you to understand. The people. The people and stories you told me about. From the bar. The guy hanging around your friend, and the motorcycle ones he gets on with, you know who I'm talking about?"

"John, what is this about? People at the bar? Really?"

"Not now! The motorcycle one you call 'Ugly' or something…you know who I mean? You know who I mean. I need him to come here. I need you to bring him here. As soon as you can. I don't care what you have to say to do it, I need you to do it."

He waited and listened, his heart pounding, thoughts of the fake suicide scene playing themselves out in his own bunk in his mind.

"John, I don't know how do that. I barely know them."

"I DON'T CARE!" he yelled. "You do it, and do it fast!" He hung up the phone, partially from nervous anger but more importantly to make a point and light a fire under her ass. She was always worried for him, and the more worried she was, the more likely she was to meet his request. *God help him if she didn't.*

CHAPTER TWENTY-SEVEN

Over a usual game of pool, Troll engaged Billy in a rare back and forth that oddly provided Billy with information he actually cared about.

"My old lady has a friend who knows a lot about the parts where you come from."

Billy chalked his que. "Is that right? Which parts are those?"

Troll, true to his name, wandered slowly around the table, eyeballing each angle on the felt. "Up there in Georgia, where the law is thick and people are getting the screws put to them left and right."

"Well, that don't sound like where I'm from, Troll.

Don't sound like it 'tall. Where I'm from, people just do what they do. Ain't much law doin' much of nuthin'."

Troll leaned down, looked over the table and stood back up, looking at Billy. "Didn't you say you were from... Winder, was it?"

Billy's heart skipped, but he made sure it was only noticeable on the inside. "I'm not sure I said...maybe I did, but yeah, 'round those parts, anyway." He took a shot at the solid on the table. He missed.

Troll, happy with a missed shot, lined his up. "Yup. Same parts. Seems some big timer got took down up there, some Dixie Mafia shit. Hatchett had those parts checked out, you know? Back when you were a newbie. He knows all about that "mafia". Those types and ours don't mix."

Billy froze. *Big-timer. Dixie Mafia. Winder...* Bates? "Hmmm, can't say I know nuthin' 'bout that."

Troll sunk the last stripe. "I was just checking. Thought you knew some people, what with all the shit you said you did and all. Guess you aren't as big as we thought."

Billy didn't take the bait. It was Troll's not so subtle way of getting Billy to say something he shouldn't. He had been a weasel like that since the day they met, and while Billy couldn't put a finger on why Troll hated him so much, he could place a big solid red checkmark on how he got his nickname with the Outlanders. Then again, *mMaybe he just forgot his skid lid one too many times*, Billy thought to himself, chuckling.

"What's so funny?"

Billy looked at Troll's ugly mug. "Ahh nuthin'. Nuthin' 'tall."

****

Billy had no way of knowing Troll had just come from a tiny room in a large prison in Georgia, where he had made a deal with the devil. John had come through in a big way, not that Dixie doubted he would after he saw him nearly piss himself at the mention of Dan's untimely demise, but he was downright tickled at the outcome of that little chat. "Troll", as they would call him, was an expedient and unexpected visitor, though he wasn't much to look at. Dixie had him pegged for a one-percenter the minute he saw him.

Through the plexi and the receiver, Dixie ranted and raved about his respect for Troll's plight, the mission of the Club, the good they all do in the world, all the while comparing what he did in Georgia to build himself up in Troll's hierarchy. Troll had already heard his name, back when Hatchett checked Billy out, and he envied Dixie's status in history as it was. Troll thought they could, or would, be friends under different geographical circumstance.

"Alright, I've damn near had enough of this place. I don't know how you do it. What is it that you went to all the trouble to get me up here for exactly?"

"You got access to sumthin' I want. Need." Dixie's face went cold. Troll almost shuddered. It wasn't quite right, the way Dixie's eyes sat in his head.

"What's that? We don't make a habit of giving shit away for free."

Dixie laughed. "Oh, I'll pay up, whatever it costs. Don't have to be money neither."

"Say it, man. I already told you, I'm sick of this... place."

Dixie locked eyes with Troll. "Billy Pierce."

Troll's insides churned the way Dixie said his name.

They usually churned at the sight of Billy, but this was sharper.

"Yup. Know him. Don't care much for him. Never have. He the reason you're in here?"

"Nah. Nah, that ain't it. Don't reckon ya need all the details. I need Billy to feel some pain. Ya understandin' me?"

"You want Billy hurt?"

Dixie smiled. "Oh yeah, I do. More than I want up out this shitbox. But not the way ya thinkin'. Take sumthin' from him. Sumthin' he cares 'bout. Take it for good."

"Help me out here. You want me to take something of Billy's away? What the fuck does that mean?"

"The girl."

Troll leaned back, coming to understanding. "Shit, man, that's a brother's little sister." He thought for a minute. "How the fuck you even know about that?"

Dixie grew agitated. "I know everything, son. Don't bother y'urself with how, unless it's you I need knowin' 'bout. Ya done come up here on y'ur own, ain't ya? Ya done said ya never liked Pierce from day one…ya wouldn't be here if ya cared that much about your 'brother' so-called."

Troll reasoned with himself that Dixie was right. And he liked the idea of it all. Billy garnered more respect with his brothers in a shorter period of time than Troll had being a prospect. His reward from this man had to be bigger than any punishment he may get were anyone to find out he was a simple go between. They would have to see Billy must deserve what he got if a man rotting in prison, leader of the Dixie Mafia, went to such great lengths to reach him and tear his life apart. It was a cruel proposition, but in line and more imaginative than Troll's norm.

"Consider it done."

Dixie smiled, his teeth worse for their wear. "I'll be seein' ya ag'in. And payin' up."

Troll shoved the chair out of his way as he stood and nodded in agreement.

CHAPTER TWENTY-EIGHT

J.J. was sitting half-ds poratop his usual rchch when the man came around the corner from the back of his house and onto the porch. "What the…" was all J.J. managed to get out before Troll interrupted him.

"Oh, just shut up and listen, you scared little peeping Tom."

"The fuck you say? Peeping Tom?" J.J. stumbled backwards, trying to get a good look at the odd-looking man in front of him.

Troll chuckled. "You heard me. I know you watch. You watch all the time. Sitting over here in your sad, little, lonely world, you watch. It's pathetic, really."

J.J. angered but guarded his words. "I can sit on my porch all I want! What the fuck am I supposed to be looking at while I'm outside? I don't remember you saying who you were?"

Troll sat on an old wooden chair and leaned back. "I'm your fairy-fuckin' Godmother, J.J."

"How do you know my name?"

"Oh, come on now. This town isn't that big, little man...especially when you go to the same bar, over and over...and over. I know why you are there."

J.J. steadied himself, not knowing if he was in any danger, but sensing he had seen this person before, having heard mention of the bar. "Slingers?"

"Mmm-hmmm," Troll said, stroking his scraggly and spotty beard.

"What about it?"

Troll leaned into the light that was shining, albeit dim, through the living room window onto the porch. His face taking a grotesque turn when he did. "What about *her*?"

J.J. inched closer to study the man's face. He did know him, he realized. He was someone Billy knew, but not a close someone. A man who rode bikes with the others who Billy knew.

"Yup, you seen me before," Troll said, reading his thoughts through his tell-all facial expressions. "You know me. So, you know what I'm about." He was giving the nod to the Club, throwing their weight in the ring, so J.J. would listen and think.

"You an Outlander?"

"Damn, you are quick on the uptake. Good God, I

170

can't believe you are the one I am counting on."

"Well. What is it that you want? What do you mean 'count on'?" J.J. asked, knowing he was pegged.

Troll nodded to the bench. "Sit down, whitey. I need a favor from you. And you might just enjoy it. Like I said, I'm granting wishes tonight, and you are one of the lucky recipients."

J.J. took a seat and listened. For twenty straight minutes, he listened. But he heard only two things. He had been chosen to "show Billy who is boss" and he would be lucky enough to "fuck that girl the way you know she wants to be fucked".

As Troll left J.J.'s porch, he left slowly, his colors showed out clear on his back, leaving no doubt for the show to follow. "You have a few days to get it done or I'll be back…and we won't be shooting the shit on the porch."

J.J. sat in thought for what seemed like hours, and as the minutes ticked by, the fear he initially felt turned into nervous energy and eventually excitement as he played it out in his mind. He felt proud of himself already. Maybe he could be part of something when he did what they told him to do. It had already become a "they". He had assumed it was a "they". But he had forgotten what happens when one assumes.

CHAPTER TWENTY-NINE

Brother startled Billy when he called. Fully asleep, barely coming to, Billy searched for his mental awareness amidst Brother's excitement. "We comin' on out Billy! Ya best git ready. Them kids 'bout goin' nuts. Give me a few days, and we'll be there, just gettin' some shit in order first."

Billy's heart felt conflicted. He was full of excitement and full of dread at the same time. "Well…a'ight then, I reckon I'll be ready." They weren't much for small talk. Never had been. He figured he best be "gettin'" some shit in order" too—in short order at that.

He fully intended to end it that night. Knowing Kathleen and the kids were coming out, he knew he had to end it. Brother had hinted at the fact there might be or had been a man in his home. He couldn't fault her, but his heart ached at the thought of it.

While the ache he felt losing, hurting, or being hurt by Kathleen had always been like pieces of his soul, cracking apart, Lacey came close. He had let himself grow with this girl. His own fault. This girl had become his girl. Also his fault. And really, he had made her into a woman beneath his hands. Like clay. And he knew he would be losing something. And she didn't know everything there was to know, and he knew that wasn't fair. But you don't start a relationship by letting someone know they probably, more than likely, don't stand a chance in the long term. And he couldn't let Kathleen go forever. He knew that from all the times he had tried before. Didn't matter what she may have done while he was gone. He, himself, was to blame for it, best he could figure.

Lacey saw him come through the doors. Noticing a slight shift in his demeanor, she walked directly to him, giving him her cherry-lipped smile. "Hi. You meeting someone?" She was so good at treating him like any other guy. Until they were alone, of course.

"Yeah, the guys are comin' up...hey I wanna talk to ya after close tonight. I'll go jack on the rocks. Keep 'em comin'."

"Please?" She smirked over her shoulder as she headed for the bar.

Damn. *Damn. This is gonna hurt.* And it was going to hurt her. *Fuck.*

He hung with the guys through the night, always watching her. "Shit, Billy, you in love with that girl or are you just a stalker? You've been watching her ass all night." He clearly didn't know.

"It's a pretty sweet ass, ain't it?"

Looking over his shoulder, the uninformed guest looked her up and down. Billy seethed. "Sure is. Wish I could get some ass like that."

If only he knew. "Yeah." And he was about to throw it all away. He had to.

The light flipped off and on, and someone shouted, "Last call. Get your drinks and your asses out of here!"

Billy ordered another drink and sat silently, watching the others file out. "I'll catch up with ya guys later." The roommates in the know chuckled.

"I got this," she said to the bartender, indicating she could close-up. The bartender looked at Billy, nodded, and tossed his rag into the sink.

"Be sure to lock up," he said, handing her the keys and looking again at Billy.

"I got it. He is fine."

"Mmm-hmmm, I know." And he was gone. And they were alone.

She pulled the blinds, locked the doors, and turned off most of the front lights. "You finish that drink. I'm going to make me one and stock the cooler right quick. Did you hear that? I'm starting to talk like you."

She was lifting a case of Michelob onto another in the walk-in when she felt his hands on her thighs, slowly raising her skirt from behind until his hands were firmly on her hips. She got lightheaded for a minute, another new sensation he gave her. His hands kept going, and she could hear his breath and feel his heated body behind her. Reaching her shoulders, he ran his hands down both of her arms until he was grasping her wrists.

"Billy," she whispered.

He raised her hands to the wall and used one hand to hold them there. She forgot they were in the walk-in cooler. She was sweating as though she had run a marathon. And she couldn't even look at him, but she knew what he looked like behind her—hungry for her, ready to take her the way he always wanted to.

Forcing her hands to stay on the wall, he traced his other hand up the inside of her legs and her raised skirt. She always went with him. He adored that about her. She trusted him, and she was willing to go.

Sliding her panties to the side he felt, again, how much he turned her on. He took her slow at first. She didn't resist. He lost himself midway and ripped her panties off, letting go of her hands on the wall and grabbing the front of her chin from behind so he could have her mouth next to his. "I love fucking you, baby."

The words always did it for her. And her excitement always did it for him. He had to hold her up as she climaxed with her arms slung back behind his neck and then leaning forward onto the cases of beer. The look of her leaning over, the shape of her ass, her torn panties on the floor, and he was epically done.

He raised her up and held her back to him, arms around her.

"I thought you wanted to *talk…*"

He couldn't. Not now. "Never mind."

"Do you want me to come over?" She picked her panties up off the ground. "I don't have any clean clothes though," she said, smiling, and gave him a quick kiss.

"Not tonight. Go on home and git some rest. I got a big day tomorrow anyway."

"Until next time," she said, creating a canyon in his

heart.

There would be no next time. And he knew it, but she didn't. *What have I done*? It was a simple question with far too complex of an answer that he would ask himself repeatedly.

****

He stayed up all night, just sitting in silence on the couch, waiting for the sun to rise and his life to come back to him. He had forgotten his life, and he grieved the part of himself he had forgotten, or at some point, simply pushed aside. He heaved the loss of his new life onto that pile of grief, a new animal inside him that had grown spiked tentacles which sunk their hooks into every internal organ he had. If he could bleed out from heartache, he wouldn't have survived the night. But the sun did rise. And he took his coffee on the front porch to catch the morning air while he waited. Any minute now, he would be looking at Kathleen and his children. He would look at them and feel love. He would look at them and feel shame. He would look at them and resent them, only slightly, for the other feelings. He knew it wasn't their fault. It never had been. It wasn't even reasonable for him to entertain the thought. But he simply wasn't reasonable, generally. Never had been for any considerable length of time. They loved him anyway. *All of them.*

He heard the sound rounding the corner. It reminded him of home. He had listened to so many roaring bikes as of late, he had forgotten the comfort he found in the purr of a solid engine. The blue beauty made its way slowly up his street to the driveway. She was a beauty, and Brother eased her in, ever so gently.

They barreled out like circus monkeys, one after the other, shoving from behind the front seats, past Kathleen, each wanting to be first to hug their daddy. They had got-

177

ten so big it hurt his heart and stung his eyes with salt. He hugged them all at once, long and hard, as they prattled on and on, over each other, to the point he didn't know who was saying what. None of them cared. They were just happy to be there. He looked up from the group hug long enough to see Kathleen standing there, waiting patiently for her turn with her husband. She looked beautiful in the morning sun. She was tired, he could tell, but she was a stunning sight to see, red cheeked and slightly thinner. He raised up from the children. "Let y'ur mama git in here now y'all. Go on in and check out the house. There's sumthin' out back for ya too." They clamored up the porch in excitement at the thought of a surprise. He stared at Kathleen. "Hi there."

She ran to him, hugging him so tight he thought she might break a rib. He held her in his worked-up arms, feeling how fragile she seemed to have become. "I'm gonna need to feed ya sumthin'. Ya seem a bit skinnier than my wife."

"Oh hush, Billy. I just been busy, same as you," she said, realizing how it sounded. They both fell silent but didn't let go. "Raising kids ain't the easiest job around."

"I know. I'm sorry, love."

"I didn't mean for ya to be sorry. I was just sayin' after work, I tend to them and then I am so tired I miss tendin' to myself sometimes, that's all."

Billy felt the pang of what was missing. "You shouldn't have to tend to them and y'urself by y'urself all the time. Don't even like the idea of ya workin', but I git it. I'm so sorry, Kathleen. I am so sorry," he said, burying his head in her hair. It smelled of strawberry shampoo and her sweet perfume, and it was soothing to his soul.

He took a step back and realized he hadn't even acknowledged Brother...or the car. "Hey there, Brother.

What say?"

Brother smiled. "Just happy to be seein' what I'm seein' 'sall."

"Well, I'm seein' that car, and I wanna see more," he said, approaching the other beauty that just rolled into his life. "Kathleen, go on ahead and check out the house with the kids. I'll be right behind ya."

She was tired and could use a cup of coffee she decided, having seen his cup on the front porch. She knew him well enough to know there was a fresh pot on inside.

"Mustang Boss?"

"Mmm-hmmm, 429 Fastback, 1970."

Billy stepped back. "Well, what are ya waitin' on? Let's bust her open and take a look, Brother!" Brother nodded and obliged.

"Likin' what you see?"

"Oh yeah, now that is sumthin'," Billy touted, inspecting the engine. "Hemi head 429 Cobra Jet Ram Air… NASCAR engine? Hooo-ey, I know what we'll be getting' into tonight!"

Brother laughed and backed Billy up. "Easy, Billy Pierce, I ain't 'bout to let ya go wreckin' my new car. Bought her just for the trip, to deliver y'ur package."

"Coop?"

"Yeah," Brother said in a way that made Billy uneasy.

"What's up 'bout that?"

Brother looked a bit sullen. "Ol' Coop. He ain't been doin' so good since Donna up and left. Hell, he wasn't right before she did. He ain't been quite right in the head for some time now. Ain't the same man. Took to drinkin' somethin' fierce. And I don't mean drinkin' to git drunk, I mean drinkin' to drink himself to death, seems."

"Donna left Coop? Well, that don't make no sense. Never knew there was problems there." Billy thought back to the odd interaction he had at Coop's just before he left town. It had been odd, sure, but not life-altering odd.

"There's a lot you been missin'. We need to talk. But let's all settle down first. We'll go for a ride later."

"Sounds a'ight," Billy said, and they headed for the house.

CHAPTER THIRTY

She was smiling and laughing as she worked her way over to him. His insides were churning. He knew that smile would evaporate the moment she realized what was happening. Happening to her. "Hey there, who we got here?"

He looked down at his cup and back up at her. He saw the smile drip slowly from her lips and the cloudiness fall across her green eyes.

"This here's my wife, Kathleen, and my daughter April. My other daughter and my boy are runnin' 'round here somewhere."

She hardened instantly. Stretching out her hand to Kathleen, she spoke softly. "Hi there, name's Lacey. I work down at the waterin' hole where these guys spend their time off..." She wouldn't look in his direction.

Kathleen thought she seemed to not care so much for Billy, and at that moment, she was probably right. "Well, that's a tough job. Bunch of sweaty guys orderin' ya around all the time? Hope Billy has been treatin' ya kind though."

"Yes, Ma'am. He has certainly done *that*. Well, it was nice meetin' ya." She couldn't remove herself quicker from his presence.

"Sweet girl," Kathleen said as Lacey walked out of his life.

He, Kathleen, and the kids stayed for several hours while the guys whooped and hollered around the fire. Lacey had left, seemingly, shortly after he had blindsided her with his family, and he felt an ache for her in his heart that he couldn't demonstrate. He couldn't have her again, and that was his punishment. And it was a harsh feeling to accept, even with Kathleen sitting right next to him.

In reality, Lacey had gone through the woods, just a short stretch, to be by the water. Where life was calm and wet ripples eased her nerves. She grabbed her stomach as she reached the shoreline and dropped to her knees on the rocks, not minding the pain. It paled in comparison to what she had just experienced. *Kids? He has kids?* Her mind wrestled through their time together, wrapped around his beautiful wife's face, and she dry heaved into the darkness. She could hear them still, the partiers. She could see the flames dancing through the woods. She thought she could even make out Billy's voice, telling stories like he always did. She closed her eyes and drew in deep breaths from the cool and magic of the water.

She splashed water on her face, and he was there. Wiping the wet away stronger from her face, she squinted up at the figure. "J.J?"

"Yeah, it's me, doll." He kneeled down, reaching out to her. She flinched and stood up. "What do you want?"

"I know, Lacey. I know what you have been up to with ol' Billy. I would bet you don't want to get into that mess with his wife. So, I have a proposition for you."

She stepped back. "You must be kidding. J.J., there is nothing in this world you have that I want, so just get on out of here and leave me be." He grabbed her wrist. Hard enough to charge her heart. "Let me be, I said! They can hear me, you know. I yell, and you'll be history." She ripped her wrist from his grasp and started back toward the woods, towards the fire.

In a split second, her face hit the rocks, and she was tasting salt and dirt. "Uhhh ohhh," he said. "Looks like you aren't going anywhere. Besides, you just busted up your pretty little face, and Billy doesn't want a whore anymore."

She gathered herself as best she could, smelling her own fear, and began to stand in front of him. "You aren't getting shit from me unless you take it, you sick piece of shit!" He smiled as she began to hand and knee run, closing in on the voices just beyond the clearing.

He caught her 5'6', 115-frame from behind and slammed her into a tree. The bark razored her lip, and she felt the heat of the blood begin to pour. He spun her around, pulled her hair back from her face forcefully, and she spit at him.

"You are a coward, J.J. Matthews. You couldn't get a girl like me if you paid for it."

"Oh, I'll be getting a girl like you. JUST like you.

And your lover boy is going be right over there", he said, motioning with his head. His breath smelled of death as he licked her entire neck.

"You disgust me," she said. And then he slammed the back of her head against the tree, and she fell to the ground.

When she woke up, he was on top of her, inside of her, smelling like booze and ripping her insides out. She put her hands weakly into his face, and he bit her fingers so hard she screamed. But her mouth had been filled with dirt and blood. Nobody to hear what he was doing, just feet from the fun. She turned her head to the side and saw a figure approaching from the way of the bonfire. *Billy?* J.J. began to shove leaves into her mouth, just in case.

He saw a glimpse of hope on her face. "You wish. You should see yourself now…not looking so pretty. Smell like a hooker too. Hey Matt, want a go at this? She is down with it. Took some convincing of course. Kind of like that Daytona gal, but she is loving it now!"

"Fuck you," she spit out in a muffle, gurgling red pieces of her soul onto his shirt.

"See, she is asking me for it. Must be good. I'll roll her over for you. This here is the sweetest ass in three counties. Not much to look at from the front anymore though."

She entered another mental space as he slapped the sense from her and rolled her face down into the leaves and dirt. Matt was on her, driving his devil into her like a madman. She felt the tearing as it happened. Everywhere. Wondering when she was going to die and why it couldn't be now. She mustered a whisper. "You will both be going to hell for this."

J.J. laughed. "Listen to the adulteress preaching up a storm."

Matt climaxed into her, onto her, and rolled off, pulling up his pants. He reached down and grabbed her ripped panties, shoving them into his pocket.

"You think we should do something with her or just leave her be right here?"

"Let her be. She isn't anything but a filthy whore in the dirt. Fuck her. Oh wait, we did that already." They both laughed. "Let's get back to the party. I feel goooood," J.J. said. "Besides, nobody will believe a two-bit slut if she tells anyone," he said, full of testosterone that clouded his mind.

Five steps later, he grabbed Matt's arm. "Hold up". He surveyed the scene beyond the trees and looked back at the heap of a once tender human covered in blood, sweat, tears, semen and dirt, and grinned like a demon. "Here's a little bit more for you, sweetheart. Just for thinking you were better than me this whole time." He chucked his beer bottle at her head as hard as he could. And she was out.

The stars swirled around her. She could still hear them, but the voices were growing faint, and the fire was going out. Literally and figuratively. She felt the shine dim from her clouded green eyes and knew her life as she had known it was over. *I want them to die*, she thought. And then she slipped away again as tears escaped her eyes that made mud trails down her once soft cheeks.

CHAPTER THIRTY-ONE

No matter how many times she had entertained the same thoughts, with question after question looming over her, she would keep the same sentiment. Kathleen knew she was different, in fact. She always knew. With anyone she even so much as entertained with a glance. And they had each come back around at least once to have what they destroyed. She wanted nothing to do with any of them. Yet, she let him return over and over. More than once. She accepted him—his want, his needs, his desire to have her, to feel her, to make sure she was still his in every way possible. He would always leave his mark in some form or fashion. And she would let him. He made her feel things she couldn't, and certainly wouldn't, feel for any other.

His eyes would pierce through her every time, and his hands melted her skin. When they actually made love, her world fell away. Both successful at hiding their "block-box", stubborn, and strong-willed, he nor she had the inclination to give in to the words, the raw emotions, and the madness they both had created in one another. So, they kept it at "love"… because it was the easiest to identify. And it felt the best. And it was true. That much they knew.

The morning was exquisite. It felt real. It felt hot. Divinely connecting. But mostly, it felt right. Somehow, they just fit into one another in all ways. When he wanted to make love to her and her to him, it was beyond ecstasy. It was slow and close and more intimate than words could express. Deep, meaningful kisses, whispers about their bodies moving in a rhythm all their own, just for each other. It always brought back memories of when they were younger, more innocent, made only for one another. A time when neither could have imagined allowing another to touch them or touching another. Simpler times. *Naivety.*

They would carry on, and the kids would have a blast on the lake until it was time for them to go.

"I miss ya so much, Billy. How long until ya come on home?"

Billy thought on the question. He missed her too. He missed Lacey at the very same moment, but in a different way. He missed his kids most of all. Sure, he had made a life and a living in the little lakefront house, but its original intended purpose had long since run its course. He had no fears of Dixie or anyone Dixie may or may not know. It would have been done by now, were it on the table. And the thought of going back home was gnawing on his brain like potato slugs in a flower patch. "I reckon I will be tyin' up loose ends here and be on your hind-tail in a short minute, Kathleen. Them kids is gettin' bigger than I ever could imagine…and it is happenin' so fast. I need to be there." His voice broke. "I ain't been there 'tall, Kathleen, and I'm sorry."

She grabbed his face, wiping his tears with her thumbs, not having memory of a time she had ever seen him cry. "It's time then, Billy. Ain't nobody comin' for ya. Ain't nobody who could. We want ya home. With us."

Billy was looking out the window down to the old makeshift dock. "My boy. He is gonna become a man 'fore long, ain't he?" He hung his head in shame.

"Yes. He is smart as a whip. Just like his daddy. And he misses you more than he could ever say, but he does say. All the time. He needs you to come home, just like the rest of us." She brought his gaze back to hers. "You 'bout done here, Billy Pierce?"

He slowly shook his head. "Yeah. I'm 'bout done here. Pack y'ur things, Kathleen, let me see ya out of town and give me a week or two, and I'll be home. For good."

She believed his words. After many years of half-truths, uncertainties, and misunderstandings, she finally and fully believed his words. The truth was in his eyes. And whatever it was he needed to clean up or finish off, she was fine with it because he would be home soon. She was sure of it.

CHAPTER THIRTY-TWO

Nobody had seen Lacey for days. She didn't show up to work, didn't answer her phone, didn't come to her door. Most knew, at this point, that seeing Billy with Kathleen had hit her hard, so they gave her space. But Whiskey Bob knew her better than anyone. They were blood, after all, and he was growing increasingly concerned over her absence. It wasn't like her. At all. Didn't matter her circumstance, she always tended to her business, keeping life as normal as possible, even when life kicked her down.

She heard his bike roar through her complex on the outskirts. She wasn't ready, and yet, she was. She had meant what she said to J.J. that night. He would be going to hell. And yes, she had wished for his death, every second since. And she wasn't sorry, which was very unlike her. But she wasn't her anymore, she figured. They killed that apologetic part of her, and that would be their own damn fault.

She unlocked the door and left it slightly open before he dismounted the bike, returning to her bed, pulling the covers up over her head.

She heard him loud and clear. "Lacey! Lace! You Here?"

He came around the corner to her room. "Lacey?"

"Yeah…" she said sheepishly from under the blanket.

"You sick or something? What's up? You got me worried sick."

She refused to show her face. The bruises were yellow-ish now, and they were not excusable by any story she could concoct…and she'd had plenty of time to run them out in her head.

"I'm fine. Go away, Bob."

He yanked the blanket and looked at her as she covered her face. Then he jerked her hands away from her face. "What…the…fuck, Lacey?" He stood up.

"Bob, sit down. It isn't what you think."

"What I think is I'm about to rearrange someone's timeline…Billy?"

She sat up, feeling the pain in her abdomen and between her legs, still, and wincing.

"Oh, heeeeelllll no. Lacey, if you don't tell me what the fuck happened here, I'm going to fuck some shit up, and I only got one man in mind."

Lacey knew he meant it. And she knew he meant to bring the others in on it too. And while she liked the idea, his anger was misdirected. And it was going to land somewhere, so she might as well speak. She had gone over it so many times in her mind, and she was right with it.

"Bob, I'm going to tell you what happened. And when. And how. But I need you to do things my way. On my terms."

"Fuck, Lacey…" he said, noticing she was unintentionally wincing and grabbing her mid-parts.

"Sit down, Bob. And listen. I need you to really listen. All the way until I'm done talking…promise me."

His face ran red, knowing whatever she was about to say was going to be epically upsetting. And clearly, downright rage-worthy.

"It happened the night of the bonfire," she started. And for once, he listened. And he didn't interrupt her or say a word until she was done recounting the horror of what the two men had done to her.

He rose slowly from her bed, backing up towards the door. "But I was there."

"Everyone was there, Bob…he liked that even more. And you know what else? He didn't even consider *you* a threat." She threw that in for good measure. And by good measure, she meant he would get it *good* what he had taken from her. "Tell Billy. I don't care how you feel about him. Tell him. Take care of it. All. Of. You."

He was stunned silent. He walked forward, kissed her forehead, and left without word. And she knew it was a matter of time before J.J. would meet the devil she only thought she had met that night. And she was fine with it. So she slept.

****

She was done with Billy. Literally, physically, and figuratively. There would never be any more telephone calls, flirting, talking, fucking, or reaching out for imaginary affection. *He would be fine with it*, she forced herself to believe. She was actually doing him a huge favor. She figured he had so many "things" to occupy his time, not to mention a wife and kids, he probably wouldn't feel one damn thing about it. Casual indifference—the opposite of love.

She felt like shattered glass had moved into her chest. *How could she have been so vulnerable, let down so many walls, done so many things she wished like hell she could take back?* It wasn't even really the things she did—she enjoyed those immensely. It was the lack of results. She had certainly been stroking his already over-inflated ego. That's what he liked. It had nothing to do with her. She was fairly certain it never had. Not even when he held her and spoke of her beauty and his love for her. And she had fallen in love with him. Easily. She had no way of knowing she was one of a string of many that would hold Billy out as the one they loved beyond all others. Lacey would place that awful feeling down deep with the other "bad things" so it would be torn to pieces by the demons that lurked there.

The darkness and deviance they gave her would remain, and it would surface again, she knew, when she could actually do something about it. She didn't expect any sense of a feeling of trust to return, but she wasn't concerned about that anymore.

People who knew her would never notice a difference in her behavior. She would do what needed to be done to get where she needed to go, but her heart, mind, and body would feel empty. Completely. The way Billy made her feel was like the immediate days after the woods. In an odd and awful way, it was metaphorically the same. And she was left a shell of a human being, struggling to breathe when nobody was watching.

She couldn't shake the feeling that, someday, they would cross paths, and it disturbed her to think about it. He didn't deserve to know what he knew about her. He didn't deserve to be anywhere near her heart or her body. She would never let it happen. She would run before she would speak a word. She hated that she still knew they could have been and were unbelievable together. It made her feel. It was the next switch to be placed in the "off" position. She was, by all accounts, a flat liner. And that is where she intended to remain until someone shocked her back to life, but the paddles wouldn't be effective for quite some time. She knew and accepted that fact as penance for making the choices she did, knowing the circumstances under which she was making them.

Billy would help Bob do what needed to be done, and *that* she could live with. It would be the perfect good-bye…given the circumstances.

CHAPTER THIRTY-THREE

Billy needed hours to overcome the news that Whiskey Bob had delivered, in none-too-subtle detail. It was the first and only time Billy actually listened to anything Whiskey Bob had to say, and he listened intently.

"Is that what she said, Whiskey? Is that what she said *exactly*?"

Bob, now her brother, looked at the floor. "Yeah, pretty much."

"Yeah pretty much, or YES?"

"Well, Billy, I mean, I'm leaving out some parts I don't really want to say. I can't."

Billy got in Bob's face. "You say them. I need to hear them. And clearly ya need to hear them ag'in."

Bob pulled up a chair. "You got a beer…or anything stronger? I'm not feeling so good."

Billy was going out of his mind, pacing back and forth. He yanked the refrigerator open and tossed Bob a beer. "Let me hear it. All of it. Every. Last. Word."

Bob drank the beer as he re-told Lacey's version of the events that transpired just beyond the clearing where they all were, a fact that was not lost on Billy. Even more so, Billy felt the realization of truth that Lacey had gone into those woods because she had just met Kathleen and the kids.

"Fuuuuuuuuuuuuckkkkkkkk!" Billy raged. "He's gotta pay, Whiskey. And I don't mean just a little, or by the measure he done. This ain't right, and he ain't right. And we're all on the hook, bein' there, knowin' him...how could this happen?" Billy felt the heat rise in his belly. "Do the others know? Hatchett?"

Whiskey shook his head. "Nah. She said tell you. You would know what to do."

It cut him. Those words she had said cut him. And they were meant to. What she was actually saying was "fix this and be gone. I am damaged forever, and you damaged me, so fix it." But he also knew her to be clear headed and kind, a thing he tended not to be when shit wasn't going his way, and this was too much for clear-headedness. It was a cloudy day at best, an entire monsoon at worst.

"Let's go, Whiskey. Hatchett needs to know. This won't stand… and he won't stand much longer." Billy knew by nickname who Hatchett was. He knew the night they met. He was a Defender—a full patch whose job is to defend a club's turf or name. He was an enforcer. And no Jolly Roger was going to soil the club by assaulting a family member and get away with it. J.J. would talk, eventually, about how he fucked Lacey and nobody did anything to him. He would get drunk and call them pussies. All things that none of them could live with, outside the fact of what had actually transpired, which sickened even Hatchett as Billy recounted to him in great detail. On purpose.

As much as Bob had not enjoyed Lacey taking up with Billy, he was on board for whatever this mission to avenge her would be. He couldn't bear the thought of what he had heard any more than Billy could, and he knew they had a love for her in common, albeit a different form.

Billy slammed the door on the way out, hoping J.J. would hear it and step outside his own door to take a peak, same as he always did. But he didn't look over to see if it had worked. He didn't care. He wanted the next time he saw J.J. to be the last time he ever saw him, and he wanted it to be even-steven. Hatchett would help make sure of it. *The sister of a "brother" and the ol' lady of a friend?* Not on this turf. Not the way they all adored her.

J.J. was a sitting duck. He didn't stray from his porch, except to go to his job, or the same bar, same as the rest of them when they weren't tending to club business at Night Moves or the clubhouse. Troll said he hadn't seen J.J. lately, and the bar confirmed neither he nor Lacey had been around for quite some time.

"Then, he is sitting at home..." Billy said to Whiskey and Hatchett. "Comfortable." The latter was directed to Whiskey.

"What the fuck are we waitin' on then?" Whiskey

replied.

Hatchett thought on it. "Let's rein it in. He isn't going anywhere. And I have an idea."

"Well it better be a downright good one 'cause I'm 'bout to go slice his nut-sack in two with any ol' object I find on the way."

They all looked up.

Billy responded. "What?"

"You are on the right track, Wild. Keep that train of thought," Hatchett said, heading towards the phone.

"What train of thought? Beatin' the livin' shit out of a rapist..." Billy trailed off at the thought of it. He became physically ill and vomited on the floor beside himself. "Fuck this shit, let's go. I'm tired of sittin' 'round lettin' him breathe the same air." He could hear Hatchett talking on the phone, catching a few words here and there, "bikes", "rope", "burn it off".

Whiskey had grown more silent than his normal personality usually allowed. He was hurting, Billy could tell. "How is she?" Billy questioned.

"She doesn't talk much. She doesn't look good... her eyes, they aren't right anymore."

Billy heaved again. *Her eyes.*

Hatchett returned to the room when he was done with the phone. "Damn boy, that's some disgusting shit," he said, referring to Billy's vomit. "Not half of what you're about to see, but damn!"

Billy got up, "So what's the plan."

"Don't you worry that pretty boy face of yours. I got this. Let's go, nighttime is coming....and nighttime is the right time."

****

He heard them coming, of course. Their bikes blazing a trail down his street. They had actually wanted him to know, and maybe even try to run. It would make the deed that much sweeter, to play a game of cat and mouse first. And he did. He tried to run, but he had been asleep before his adrenaline kicked in, and the war wagon quickly and easily cut him off on the sidewalk. It was overkill, really, bringing the beast on this particular mission, but a few extra hands and little bit of extra firepower just in case, seemed appropriate enough. Besides, they needed a place to throw their mouse once they caught him...and maybe bat him around a little before they got where they were going. It would be a fun ride.

After his arms were tethered to the bridge post, they each took their turns with him— talking, spitting, kicking, or worse.

Billy knelt down next to him. "You know what I don't git? What made a dickless, cunt boy like you think ya could do something like this for *one*, and how possessed were you with the first pussy you ever felt, by force mind ya, that ya thought ya was gonna git away with it? In this crowd too!" Billy spat at him, almost laughing, while J.J. cried. "Cry all ya want, BITCH!" Billy said, kicking him as hard as he could in the ribs before spinning on his heel. "Might make ya feel better knowin' ya ain't the only one. Y'ur buddy Matt is next up," he said, walking away, nodding to Whiskey to make the call.

Whiskey threw a leather gloved finger in the air,

201

like he was giving the number one signal while everyone watched, and J.J. went silent, clothes soaked through with the booze the men had spat on him and the urine he had released on himself in fear. And then, Whiskey's finger started to turn in a circular motion, around and around. On that command, Hawk began to back his bike up ever so slowly, heading straight for the middle of J.J.'s legs—strung to and steadied by bikes ridden by Chug and Tattoo Dusty.

"No! No! You guys have this all wrong. Please! Your guy told me to do this! I thought I had to! Troll threatened me! I had to!"

It was then that Billy noticed Troll was absent. And so did everyone else. But it only hit them briefly through their rage and blood lust. Then, it was gone.

J.J. began to scream when he realized what was happening, actually. He had first thought they meant to scare him. But the Outlanders didn't fuck around and play Halloween games. He was going to get what he gave…and then some.

The smell of the burning rubber and flesh was sickening and gratifying all at once. As long as Whiskey kept turning that finger, Hawk would keep the rubber grinding down what was once J.J.'s manhood. And Whiskey wouldn't stop, thoughts of what J.J. had done to Lacey racing through his mind. They all knew it. And it bothered none. Through the pain, the smell, the screams, and the smoke, eventually J.J. passed out.

Hatchett looked to Billy. "That's probably enough blood to bleed out slow enough but for sure, right?" It was almost a joke, coming from a man with a nickname like "Hatchett".

They fully intended to leave J.J. there with his mutilated genitals to bleed out. He may have come to or may not have, but he would not be getting help, and he would definitely be dying feeling excruciating pain in his dick, or the area where his dick and balls should have been—the only things he owned that ever made him feel like anything at all resembling a man in this world. Whiskey would stay to make sure of it. And to get rid of the waste.

There had clearly been some sort of tent city under that bridge, judging by the barrels and the trash, and the night was growing chillier every second. One last barrel fire, and everyone would warm up on the inside.

****

Back at the club, without Billy who had been asked to leave, nobody spoke. They all went over the one thing J.J. had said that meant anything to them at all. Troll.

"Anyone going to say anything?" Hatchett asked.

Whiskey Bob knew what he meant. "You think that was real? Troll is a pain in the ass, but a fuck-over like that? Why would he? He *is* aware of the hell that would rain down on him if this were something he had done."

They all nodded in agreement, having seen the consequences of crossing a brother or the Club before.

Henry-Nine piped in. "I don't know, but I do wonder… why would Troll's ugly mug be on his mind when he had a nasty, steaming pile of rubber coming towards his nuts? He's the last fucking thing I would be thinking about."

Hatchett looked to the others. "Maybe it was the

only thing he could think of...any of you got any answers?"

Whiskey Bob and Tattoo Dusty looked at each other.

"What? You got something to say, you say it!" Hatchett demanded.

Tattoo Dusty pushed past Whiskey Bob. "Troll went out of town not a few weeks ago. He never said where he was going or why...just kind of left. When he got back, he was...different...happy almost. Thought he took himself a vacation and maybe got him some. But he never said. And I thought, for him, that was strange. He *is* Troll."

"Likes to talk," Hatchett said. "Surely would do some talking about any ass he may have gotten and made up a few along the way."

Hatchett made motion to Henry-Nine and Chug. "Call him in boys. We need answers. Whiskey, that story true?"

Whiskey looked down, in shame, realizing he may have missed the signs that led to his sister's undoing, "Yeah, he is right. Troll took off."

Hatchett took to preaching. "If, in fact, what J.J. no-nuts said is the truth, then Troll has broken our bylaws and code of conduct." And he rattled a few of them off. "No member will disgrace the club by being yellow. No member will take the attitude that he doesn't have to help other members, and other members don't have to help him. No member will go against anything the club has voted for and passed. No member will get together on their own and plan something for themselves. It will be brought up to the whole club and the whole club will participate in anything that is decided upon. Is this something any of you decided upon?" Hatchett asked, looking squarely at Whiskey Bob.

All responded in unison, "No sir."

"I figured not. Well then, let's see what Troll has to say, shall we? But let's give it some time to rest and to fester. He has outside interests and ties to shit we don't want any part of. Hear me? Let. It. Rest. Leave it to *me*."

They all voiced their agreement and obligation.

CHAPTER THIRTY-FOUR

"I gotta be getting' back to where I belong now. Ain't nuthin' I need knowin' here," Billy said to Hatchett and Niner at his dining room table.

They understood what he meant. They didn't judge his sins in the meantime. "It's been something," Hatchett said.

Niner agreed. "Yeah, it's been *sumthin*'," he said, mocking Billy's unchanged way of speaking.

"I tell ya what, if the two of ya ever quit tryin' to talk like me, that'll be the day." They all laughed together. "Hey, Niner, I don't mean no disrespect, but I been wonderin' 'bout that missin' finger of y'urs since the night I met ya!"

"Well, hell, Billy, all you had to do was ask. No, wait. If you would have asked the first night, you would be Billy Nine by now," he followed. "I lost it gambling."

"Gambling…" Billy pondered. "What kind of a bet ya make?

"The ring on my finger, except when it came time to pay up, it wouldn't come off, so I squared up."

"Holy hell, ain't that some shit. Ya may not be right in the head," Billy responded. "I would know!"

Hatchett laughed a hearty laugh at the two of them. "Let's place some bets now, boys. One last go?"

Billy was on the way out. He couldn't help himself. *What's a few extra dollars or a few dollars less*, he thought, until he realized he could lose a non-numerical digit between these two. They went to the nearest sports hole. Everyone watched them walk in and through, the leathers giving them a stir. Billy went straight to the board in the back, checked out what was on deck, and remembered the bet he had placed so many years before, when Dixie was teaching him to dabble, and he jumped in head first.

"What'll it be," the unofficial boss asked.

"College ball. National Championship," Billy replied. "I'll take Oklahoma over Penn State."

The boss laughed. "That's a freshman quarterback, son."

Hatchett chimed in. "Even I know that. That's a sorry wager there, slick."

"Don't care," Billy said and threw down a hundred.

"Alright. Hundred on Oklahoma it is. Just in time, too."

Billy sank into the regular booth with Hatchett and Niner and watched his money make itself on the television behind the bar.

"I guess I better pay up," Hatchett said, standing up.

"You plannin' on runnin'," Billy laughed.

Hatchett gave him a nod, the kind Billy came to know as "this way" in the silent way Hatchett and Club communicated. Billy shook Niner's hand in a solid, appreciative gesture as he left.

"Oh boy, what ya gone and done this time?" Billy said, knowing money wasn't the payment plan.

Outside the bar, next to Hatchett's bike, was a Harley Davidson trike, without a speck of dust on her. *Ghosted again*, Billy thought. "That ain't mine…" he trailed off, getting goosebumps at the sight of it.

"Well, I figured you love your four wheels, and you love your two wheels. Why not find your in between? Plus, I have seen the way you look at them."

They laughed together. Billy realized they had become true friends and there would never be anything that would change it. "Damn, Hatchett, y'ur sumthin else, my friend."

"Look who's talkin'…free ridin' hell on wheels. Keep it on straight, Billy boy. We will take care of what needs taking care of."

Billy's heart broke. Lacey. J.J. had paid. Troll had yet to square up.

Hatchett saw the broken and tormented look on Billy's face. "You know where to find me if you need me. Now, get on out of here before you start crying like a baby. Leave the other," he said, referring to the shovelhead that had taken Billy's virginity and run away with it screaming. He had never upgraded or felt the need to. Besides, it had been a gift.

He would let her go for the trike like she was nothing. Billy held out his hand, and Hatchett shook it firm. They both lingered for a moment, and then Hatchett turned to go, throwing a hand up over his shoulder in final gesture as he did.

Billy had planned to sleep in the motel where he had begun his Jacksonville jag that night and head for home at daybreak, figuring it too cold to hit the open road, especially in the middle of the night. But he drove all night, skin covered as best it could be, and the air washed over him, as if to cleanse him of where he had been. Or maybe, what he had done.

As he drove through Jasper, he saw a giant structure in the beginning phases of life. He wondered what they would build that was so large in such a small place and why. He reckoned it must be a military facility of some sort or maybe even a prison. *Prison.* The thought sent a shudder through him as he thought again of Dixie. Rotting away in a cell at what he knew as the Georgia Diagnostics and Corrections State prison or GDCP, *for short. Short...* the man Dixie had made "disappear" for him. Too much irony, too many memories.

Dixie had already beaten the system most of his life, and he had definitely beaten the legal system in short order. Who was to say he wouldn't beat those bars entirely and walk down the same old streets he used to walk down when things were the way they were, before everything went to shit on a shingle? And the closer Billy got to what was once his home, the more he thought of that very thing—the day Dixie would walk free, if it ever came. And Billy was almost certain it would. *And that would be a very, very bad day.*

Billy needed a mental break, and he had one last stop in mind before he made it home. He watched for the lights and the words and pulled over the minute he saw one blazing, "Tattoos". He didn't care who it was or what kind of experience they had, artistically. It was the thought and the pain he sought.

"What'll it be fella?" The tatted-up man said as he emerged from the back room, hearing the bell.

"I'm ready to go when you are. Free hand is a'ight. I know what I want."

"Well, give me some idea, and we'll get it goin' then."

Billy raised his pant leg, circled the area around the side of his calf and described the green-eyed, perfect bodied girl with golden hair he wanted kissing an eight ball with the curve of her lower back fully in view.

"Nice. I like it," the artist said. "Let's go then."

Billy walked out with exactly what he wanted. Yet every time he looked at it, she was a green-eyed devil, slamming her pitchfork into his heart. But she would be there forever, for good or for bad, and he meant to feel those feelings, both the good and the bad. She would have to, so he would force himself. *Consequences.*

"Even though I walk through the valley of the shadow of death, I will fear no evil…"

~Psalm 23:4

CHAPTER THIRTY-FIVE

When he pulled into the drive, the house was dark. He had expected lights and laughter and smiles, maybe even a homemade "welcome home" sign from Buddy. He had grown more excited the closer he got to Winder, knowing Buddy would go crazy for his three-wheeler. He couldn't wait to take the girls for a ride, one at a time. But nobody was home. Not one person there to greet him, to hug him, to let him know he had been missed. She had warned him. He hadn't listened.

"Things ain't the same, Billy. I ain't the same," she had said in Florida, just before she filled him in on her new life. And he sat there and listened. He listened, tormented by the way she simply put it out there—the truth. He had left, and it had been more than a moment. And he could have come home a long time ago, but he chose not to, and she knew it. She was up to her neck in quicksand with the kids, especially Jo, and they needed a father figure, not the shadow of a man who once was and may or may not be again. She was lonely and tired of being the entire family, for everyone. "We been spendin' most our time with Dale."

"So, it *is* Dale Duncan. Damnit, Kathleen, you sure know how to pick 'em." He couldn't help his anger that gained momentum as he listened.

"What's that s'posed to mean comin' from you?"

He threw the table over as he stood up. "What's *that* s'posed to mean?"

She looked at him with eyes he didn't recognize. They were tired and unafraid. "Ya know damn well what it means."

"Ya takin' my kids away, Kathleen? Ya leavin' me for good?"

"Don't have to, you a'ready did," she said matter-of-factly as she got up and went outside.

Minutes ticked by as she stood in the fresh air, settled in her new-found dignity, listening to pieces of his Florida life shatter or break in the tornado of his anger. The house grew silent, and she heard the door open behind her. "I got one question left."

"Fine."

He walked up beside her, and without looking at her, asked the wind, "Do ya still love me, Kathleen?"

She looked down at the ground, hands making their way to her face, and wilted slowly down to the porch. She sat in silence for a brief moment. "Ya know I do. Can't hardly say why. Don't even know ya anymore. But I still do."

"A'ight then," he said, satisfied. And that was that. He didn't fill her in on what he knew of Dale Duncan. He knew she would figure it out for herself. But he did swear to himself that he would fill Dale in on Billy and Kathleen Pierce.

When he realized that she and the kids were, in fact, at Dale's when he got home, the reality of it hit him square in the gut. He had nothing, it seemed. And the funny thing about it was, he hadn't had a damn thing without them for quite some time. He was just now realizing it, standing outside his house. As he took what few possessions he had inside, he figured he would go ahead and get rip-roaring drunk while he was alone and set things right the next day. He had a mind to call Brother and get straight to kicking asses, but he was damn tired, from his biking boots to the heart on his sleeve. He passed out in Buddy's room next to a picture of himself that sat in a wooden frame on Buddy's bedside table. He gazed at himself casting a line in a small pond they used to frequent, cigarette hanging from his lip.

The next day, he set off early to get what he needed. He would watch and wait outside Freightliner until he could corner the man that was in his way. He was halfway through a strong cup of coffee from the convenience store when they drove up together. His blood began to boil. *Keep it steady*, he said to himself. She went inside without him, seeming to pay no attention to the person who had driven her to work. They weren't getting' on, best he could tell. Dale sat in the car for a good minute before he got out. Billy dismounted the trike, camouflaged by the trees between lots, and started towards him. When Dale picked up speed towards the side door, Billy had to make a verbal move. "Hey!"

Dale stopped dead in his tracks, as if he knew. He turned to find Billy closing in quickly. "Billy Pierce. Why am I not surprised?"

"Ya ain't surprised because that's my wife ya brought to work. And ya know me."

It was a true statement. Dale did know Billy. He had said that exact thing to Kathleen, but she hadn't read into it beyond face value. "What is this exactly, Billy? Ya come here to tell me sumthin' I don't know yet? Oh, I know. I'm fuckin' y'ur wife, remember?" he said wryly.

He had tested and turned the beast in Billy. "Ya best watch y'ur mouth. And mind y'ur business. Go find y'ur own. Or y'ull be findin' y'urself in a right mess."

Dale dismissed him. "I ain't scared of ya, Billy. Y'ur buddies ain't 'round no more, and last I heard, ya done got run out like a scared little kid."

"Keep thinkin' that," Billy said as he turned to leave Dale with his words. He stopped and turned to throw one last line in the sand. "She's still wearin' my ring, ain't she?"

Dale felt the kick in his stomach but acted like it meant nothing to him as he swung open the door to the building and went inside. He would add a little kick of his own to his coffee five minutes later. The self-soothing wouldn't stop all day. Dale would keep drinking coffee all day that day, and it would get stronger and stronger until it wasn't coffee anymore. Kathleen didn't see Dale all day, which was an oddity given their schedules in the building, but she was minding her own anyway since she had returned from her trip. He was nowhere to be found when it was time to go home, and she cornered a co-worker to take her home, to *her* home, for the night.

In truth, Dale had avoided her, his anger and the alcohol having seeped into his bones. And she would be lucky for it.

He didn't see the cargo van until it was too late.

Kathleen had to sift through the shock of Billy's return and the promises she had made Dale, and ultimately ran to his bedside in the early morning when the hospital contacted her.

****

Some people turn into better versions of themselves having gone through life-changing events. It's like they wake up new. Mentally, they truly and completely wake up to life. That wasn't the case for Dale. He did wake up new, that much she could say, but he woke up newly angry, newly bitter, and newly violent. God had cheated him, he would say as often as he could.

She would try to remind him that he lived, and if anything, that was a gift from God, but the mere mention of silver linings enraged him. He wasn't a man anymore, by his estimation, and if he wasn't a man, what good was he? Attached to a chair, unable to function of his own accord, unable to walk, feel, fuck, or fight. To Dale, the accident had been a death, and he would mourn himself all day, every day. And he would grow increasingly tired of Kathleen hanging around, convincing himself she was there because she felt she had to be, not because she had a kind heart or any true feelings for him. So, her help was unwelcome, but her absence was not an option. He didn't care how his anger, drinking, or violence affected her because for him, no matter what, things were ten times worse. While she said her prayers each night, he said his "damn you-s".

219

CHAPTER THIRTY-SIX

When a shotgun blasts into a person's ife, the shrap-
nel goes everywhere. It sticks, and it bleeds, and it stings...
even after it doesn't. People in the kill-zone remember every little detail from the pull of the trigger—the lead up, the
event, the after-math. It all seems to take up so much time.
In reality, real-time, the here and the now, truly bad things
happen in an instant.

Dale told them Kathleen had eaten her dinner, said
she was tired, gotten up from the dinner table, and started
to walk to the sink to wash her dish when she collapsed.
Within minutes, she had died. Right there. No warning,
no cause, no explanation, save the "hadn't been feelin'
well for weeks". Or so he said, anyway. He didn't want to
"waste money on an autopsy since she was sick," leaving

no room for debate. As her husband, he decided on his own to have her cremated. Everyone disagreed with his version of events and the decisions to follow but had no standing to object, despite their desires.

Buddy knew better. Buddy had always known what kind of man Dale was. No matter what people said or didn't say, Buddy could read people like a book. It was a gift, really. It didn't stop him from keeping bad people around, but he always knew where they stood, mentally, and Dale Duncan was dark on the inside, especially when he wasn't getting his way. And in this instance, his way was about to be diverted something fierce. And he knew it.

Circumstance and heartache had taken their toll on Kathleen, for sure. The fire in her soul that lit her life-light had grown dim, if it had not been snuffed out completely. Where once there was hope, even a slight glimmer, guiding her steps, now there was nothing but drudgery. She became world-weary and unaffected. "Should-haves" and "would-haves" plagued her thoughts unabated. When they would take over, she would attempt to push them aside, knowing the uselessness of their consideration. Life was what it was anymore, and there didn't seem to be a damn thing Kathleen could do about it. She sure couldn't help Dale. And she grew tired of the strife.

Dale had overheard Kathleen talking on the phone to Billy late one evening, which wasn't an odd occurrence. They had kids together after all, but this conversation was different. And she was different. Since the day she came home from the family reunion, she had been different towards him. He would give her the fact that he hadn't always been the nicest man to her or the most loving husband, and damned if he wasn't a pain in the ass to care for since he lost the use of his legs, but he couldn't see that it made more of a difference to her than to him. It was *his* life, after all. *His* legs, *his* manhood that were gone forever.

Not hers. He just couldn't see it that way. And the more he tried, the angrier he got. He knew it wasn't her fault, but she was there, and she should be able to bear his pain just the same.

That night on the phone, in a hushed tone, she talked about her plans, the most of which he could not hear past his own wrath once he realized she planned to leave him for good. And not just leave him. Leave him for Billy. Go back to Billy, again. She would choose Billy over him, the man who had broken her so, taken her legs out from under her just as sure as his were gone by other means. Billy had clipped her wings. And she still preferred *him*.

"No," he muttered and rolled his chair out to the dining room. "Won't be having this," he said to stale, empty air in their cluttered home. He looked around, feeling empty of anything but anger. Truth be told, he had nothing but anger in him since the accident. At first, he thought it would make him a better man. It never came around to that, and he turned bitter and cold on the inside, blaming everyone and anyone who would come within earshot. Ending up with Kathleen as the only sounding board. And now she wanted to leave. She was leaving. He had heard her say as much. And he would be all alone. And he wasn't going to sit idly by and let this happen *to* him. Again. So much had happened *to* him. Not anymore. He would take over the situation. He would be in charge. He *needed* to be. It was decided before he even did his research.

It didn't help anyone but Dale that he was former security with police officer training. Right there in that county. He knew things that the average person didn't, especially the average person where they lived. She had been ill in one way or another for practically her entire life, another bonus were he to follow through. It was an easy sell to his brain. His heart didn't factor because it had died along with the use of his legs. He would make it easy for her though. She had done right by him the best she knew how under what he would consider not exactly the best of circumstances, but certainly not the worst. But he would do right by himself also, making sure he could live out his own days in what he considered peace, not having to watch the only woman who would ever care for him in the state he was in, take back up with a man he subconsciously considered to be his superior in every way possible. He'd spent far too much time convincing himself consciously he was quite the opposite.

To be sure, he *let* himself feel the envy of Billy's vitality, his vigor, his wild nature. He called it "stupidity", the way Billy rambled on in life like a juiced up young version of himself, always living his "Wild" life, yet always providing for what needed providing for. Dale ranted about it to Kathleen every chance he got.

While Dale pondered the ways in which he could accomplish his final marital task, he envied. More than anything, he envied Billy. He reasoned that he would *save* her, save *himself* the agony of what was to come, and cut the man who planned to ruin his life so deeply that he may *never* recover. It all seemed common-sensical to Dale. It would become his resolution. And for Dale, resolve was never an issue.

He called their house in a frenzy. April answered. He told her that Kathleen had collapsed and was in the emergency room. In a frantic, frenzied state, April found Jo and Jamie and rushed to the hospital.

While they waited for news, Dale recounted the story. The doctors emerged in no time with the most tragic news of any of their lives. She was gone. Within minutes, she had died, they figured. Right there in Dale's kitchen. The ambulance to the hospital had been a formality.

Buddy knew better.

****

April opened the door and waited for her dad to get to the porch. It was more than a shockwave that swept through Billy's core. In a sense, it was as though Billy was experiencing his own death. He felt his insides melting into pools of despair, and his outsides crumbled as well. Wilting to his knees, Billy raised his hands to his face and wailed as though Satan, himself, had appeared before him for roll call.

"What are ya sayin' to me right now…what are ya' sayin'?"

April stared numbly at the ground. "She is gone now, Daddy. She is gone."

Billy looked up, hoping to find any semblance of possibility that April was misinformed, or better yet, that he was dreaming. He had dreamt this very thing before, more than once. "April, tell me now, is this real? Am I dreamin'? Am I livin' right now or dyin'?"

"Daddy, you are livin', and this ain't goin' away." And then it hit her. Square in the chest and her increasingly enormous heart-space. Rising from her gut like a tidal wave of smothering ash, she began dry heaving the breakfast she couldn't eat. She leaned on Billy's shoulder and then fell to her knees and grabbed him with both arms for comfort.

"Tell my boy."

"I don't know where he is right now, Daddy."

Billy looked April in the eyes, held her shoulders, and sturdied himself. "Ya find my boy and tell him. Then send him to me."

April shook her head in acknowledgment and tried to pick herself up off the ground. She felt like a thousand pounds of bricks were weighing her down and her heart would certainly fail her at any moment and it would be over. This day, this thought, this reality, this nightmare she had woken up to, would be over. It, however, was only beginning, and she knew that too.

CHAPTER THIRTY-SEVEN

Billy put Willie Nelson's "Angel Flying to Close to the Ground" on the record player to soothe his soul and absorb the feelings of the angel he had loved for what seemed like his entire life. The same night, Kathleen came to him. He was in and out of fitful bouts of sleep when she walked through the door in his old shirt and some faded blue jeans. Always his favorite outfit on her. She had a smile on her face that was serene and beautiful, the same smile that used to light up the world, his world. She sat down right in front of him.

"Hi, Baby," she whispered, reaching a hand out to brush his hair away from his sweaty brow.

"Kathleen?" Billy sat up with a heart rush.

She looked him up and down. "Ya ain't lookin' so good, Billy."

"Kathleen, ya ain't really here, are ya?"

She smiled an easy, knowing smile. "You can see me, can't ya?" She leaned in and kissed him gently on the lips. "Ya feel that, don't ya?"

He felt a jolt of electricity, that much was for sure. "Yeah. I see ya. I feel ya. But I reckon I know better."

She grasped his hands lightly, and a hint of sorrow swept across her face. "Ya never did know what ya knew, Billy."

He knew exactly what she meant. Knowing things never meant a damn to him when it came to doing things. He wished he could make sense of what was happening. "I'm sorry, Baby, for all the things...."

"No. Don't ya go doin' that. It's all nuthin' now. All that matters is love. And I love you. And I love my kids. And I know that things are gonna be just fine."

He felt her confidence. "But Kathleen, how can we be, I mean live, without ya?" A tear escaped amid his weariness.

Kathleen leaned close to Billy and placed her cheek on his cheek, feeling the warmth of the salty drop that had escaped from the eyes she knew so well, and whispered, "You will never be without me, Sweetheart. I'm every-where, forever...especially right here." She placed both of her palms over his heart, and then she was gone.

Billy struggled to find reality. He rubbed his eyes, slapped his face, and blinked hard a couple of times before getting onto his feet to brew some coffee. If none of it was real, how could he have felt so awake the entire time? He went over it in his mind and touched his cheek where hers had been—*still wet.* He paced the floor and replayed the conversation he had just had with his beloved Kathleen, recorded word for word in his mind with sharp clarity, while his coffee-maker gurgled. His heart ached at the thought of her hands on his chest, and he pulled his shirt to his face to recapture an ounce of the dream of her presence. And there, he smelled her soft fragrance. *Still beautiful.*

Comfort swept over Billy in those dim morning hours as he realized he knew something to be true. Kathleen knew he loved her more than anything in the world. Kathleen forgave him of all things. Kathleen loved him. Kathleen was at peace. And so was he. This time, he "knew what he knew".

April, Jo and Buddy would feel, see, and *know* it differently. So would Dixie.

****

229

EPILOGUE

James Bates, Inmate Number 36661
Georgia Diagnostic and Classification Prison
Highway 36 West
Jackson, GA 30233

Billy Boy,

I reckon ya been thinkin' on this now most y'ur
life, we old men. Has it been a riddle to ya, or
have ya figured it out by now?

Y'ur whore down in Florida—that was me. Y'ur
pretty little wife, mother of your children—that
was me too. The last one though, that one's
on you. Damn. Makes ya kind of wonder what
kind of man ya been, doesn't it? I tried to
teach ya what I knew, but ya never could quite
listen, could ya?

I bet right now ya got a sick feeling deep down
inside y'ur gut you can't get hold of. Maybe ya
ain't sick at all. Maybe ya ragin' like I been all
these years. 'Cept ya been out there, while I
been in here.

I been thinkin' we should talk about it. I'll be
seeing ya soon to git that taken care of.

Take care now.

Dixie

ABOUT THE AUTHOR

Sybil Watters is the daughter of Swiss immigrants and an "Okie" by birth. Watters is a practicing attorney with a lifelong love for reading and writing fiction. Watters has written numerous articles and short stories on various topics of interest to include the law, "chic-lit", paranormal fantasy and satirical pop-culture. She is a regular guest post author on many blog sites.

Watters's current project, The DIXIE Series, is gritty, new-adult, deep-south fiction, a region for which Watters has a passionate fascination. DIXIE, Book One: Open Roads was released to critical acclaim nationwide for Watters's authentic use of southern slang and true-to-life, young-adult angst amidst a tumultuous time and venue. DIXIE, Book One: Open Roads is avaie now on Amazon and www.dixiebookseries.com. Watters now releases the highly-anticipated sequel, DIXIE, Book Two: Ramble On with accompanying DIXIE merchandise and the epic finale of the series DIXIE, Book Three: Born & Bred is shortly to follow in 2019.

Watters practices law, lives, and writes quietly in the mountains with her husband and four rescue dogs.

Masterfully crafted by Sybil Watters, "DIXIE, Book One: Open Roads" perfectly captures the culture, people and struggles of the Deep South as it was forty years ago. This compelling new series twists fact and fiction to tell the story of a troubled young man who, while he has his family's best interests at heart, is forced to struggle with haunting demons that often choose immorality over integrity. Everything collides into a thick cocktail of suspense that is garnering critical acclaim from coast to coast as a "redneck revolution" sweeps the nation.

**"DIXIE Book One: Open Roads" is available
nationwide on all major electronic outlets
and also via: www.facebook.com/sybilwatters**